THE CALL OF KAREN

DENISE LYNN LAMBERT

To my daughters, Myndi and Valerie. You know why.

Prologue: The Land of the Great Old Ones

"Does this look normal to you?" Cthulhu stood, dripping wet, having emerged from the lukewarm water into the hot and sticky air of Lovecraft Lake.

"Eww, put that away," Cthalhay said. "Why did you show me that?"

"Well, I have to ask someone. I don't want to eat it if it's not going to be good." In his hand he held a fish-like creature with two heads and an extra tail protruding from the side of its body. One of the heads had three eyes.

Cthalhay shook her head. "Well, first, you should not show such things to your sister. Second, it looks abnormal, but the same kind of abnormal as the other fish in this lake, so I wouldn't worry about it."

Cthulhu shrugged, and shoved the squirming creature past the tentacles surrounding his mouth. A crunch muffled by squishy chewing sounds followed. He wiped his webbed hand on his swim trunks, then crossed his arms and belched.

"How are things with Idh-yaa and the kids?"

Cthulhu sighed, and the green tentacles covering his mouth fluttered in the breeze of his fish-laden breath. "Well, now that the kids are off to college, we have the house to ourselves."

"Empty nesters. How's that going?" Cthalhay put her hand on her hip and smiled.

"Why do I have the feeling you already know the answer to that?"

"Whatever your feeling, how about you just answer the question?"

"We're getting a divorce. At least I think so."

"I didn't think that was possible here. How do the Great Old One's feel about that?"

"Everyone but Elhort is okay with it, really. I mean, we don't have real cause per se, although I do wonder sometimes if she has a wandering eye. I have let myself go a bit." He patted his green belly, protruding more than it had even a few years ago. Turning 1500 did that to you, or so some people said.

"What's she saying?"

"Well, when the kids were in the house, I always had them to blame for things. You know, leaving the skulls of our enemies in the sink and not putting them in the dishwasher, stuff like that. It was me all along, and I hate to think of the lashing those kids took for things I did."

"That's seems pretty mild. Why don't you just do better?"

"I try, but nothing seems to be good enough. I think she misses disciplining the kids, and so I am the next best thing."

"C'mon Cthulhu. We've known each other our whole lives. You can be honest with me."

"You really want to know? Because I think it is pretty funny actually."

"What is it?"

"Well, the other night I got up in the middle of the night to—well, you know. Happens way to often lately." He needed to get his prostate checked, but he dreaded the visit to his doctor. He had fingers that were both long and fat. He shuddered.

"So. What did you do, wake her up?"

"Well, not exactly. She's always on me to put the toilet seat down, and I have been doing pretty good, but I decided it just wasn't doing it. I left it up on purpose."

"You didn't!"

"You know me. Never shying away from a little mischief."

"What happened?"

"I heard the splash first, then the screams. I woke up with a pillow over my face. She was trying to kill me."

"Not true. If she was trying, you'd be dead."

"Perhaps true. Anyway, she let me live, but told me to leave, she was filing for divorce."

"How long ago?"

"Two weeks."

"Where have you been staying?"

Cthulhu pointed to a sad looking tent in a muddy clearing between two large, twisted trees.

"What have you been eating?"

In response, he belched loudly, licked his lips and swallowed.

"Oh, no. This won't do. You're coming to my house. You can stay with me."

His sister had a tiny place. She'd never married, much to the disappointment of the Great Old Ones and the up and coming Mediocre Young Ones.

But Cthulhu hated imposing, and he liked being alone. Mostly. "I can—"

He didn't get a chance to finish. A large limb broke loose from one of the trees and fell, landing squarely on the top of his tent. He looked back to find Cthalhay smiling.

"Well, maybe for a couple of days. I was thinking of taking a vacation anyway."

"Where to?"

"Delaware."

"Isn't that—"

"On earth?" he finished for her. "Yes."

"Aw, don't you remember what happened last time?"

"Yeah, but people feel differently about the Great Old Ones now. Me in particular. Hang on."

Cthulhu ran to his destroyed campsite, grabbing what clothing he could, along with his cell phone. Ever since the Land of the Great Old Ones got 5G, the world had changed, for the better he thought.

He pulled a shirt on over his bulging, slimy chest, and touched the screen to bring it to life. He logged into Facebook and pulled up a photo. He tapped it and enlarged it, then turned the screen her way.

"Cthulhu for President, 2024" the photo said. Under his name was a slogan: "Why choose the lesser evil?"

"See?" Cthulhu said. "They want me to be their leader."

"Are you sure that isn't some kind of joke?"

"No. But I intend to find out. And if it is…" he pounded one webbed fist into the other and growled. "Then I will use my vacation to create havoc."

"Why Delaware?"

"Delaware Bay to be exact. Look" He tapped the maps app on his phone and showed her.

"Very nice. Looks like a mouth about to swallow ships."

Cthulhu grinned. "Exactly."

"Do the old ones know you are going?"

Cthulhu shook his head. His tentacles continued to wave even after he stopped.

"You know they will pursue you, right?"

"Not if they don't know I'm gone."

Cthalhay sighed. "All right. I'll help. C'mon. Let's get you cleaned up and fed before you head out."

Cthulhu took her offered hand and walked away from the lake and his makeshift home. He grumbled as he did. After all, complaining and causing trouble were his superpowers. That, and being the epitome of evil.

He couldn't wait to get to earth. Delaware wouldn't know what hit it.

ONE

Crossing Delaware

THE STATE OF KANSAS, 2023

"Is there some kind of award for that?" The aluminum can lay on the fencepost, cut in half. He coiled his whip and put his hat back on his head, straightening it and tapping it into place.

"Nope. But that is impressive." The balding man stared at him. "You sure you want to do this?"

"Look, I'm bored as hell. The last treasure I hunted was some rumored bullion some billionaire asshole was supposedly hiding in Florida. Nothing. Since then, business has been slow, and I am running low on both cash and excitement."

"The wife has you on a short leash, eh?" When the bald man laughed, everything on his body jiggled. He stared up at Kansas, and one of this three chins disappeared. "That your real name?"

"I don't have a wife. And yeah. My dad wasn't really creative, and my mom was passed out when he filled out the birth certificate."

"Ever think of changing it? I mean, it's kinda like…" the bald man trailed off as Kansas gave him the meanest stare he could.

"Don't say it," he said.

"But—"

Kansas held up the whip. "I'm aware of what you are saying, but not saying. You want to keep it that way."

"O-o-okay. So we start Friday nights at seven. You go on at eight, after the gunslinging show. Remember, no one really gets hurt, except for the midget from time to time. You'd think he would hit the barrel just right after all that practice."

"How much?"

"Fifty a night plus tips. Most performers get plenty, go home with a couple hundred. You'll probably do great. Especially with the ladies." The bald man raised what should have been eyebrows but were really hairy furrows on a fatty forehead. The man had fat cells where it didn't seem humanly possible.

"Okay. And you are?"

"Colin."

"And it's cash, right?"

"Yep."

Just as they finished talking, a chirp sounded in Kansas' pocket. He pulled his phone free.

"Smith here," he answered the unknown number.

"Kansas Smith?" The voice on the other end of the line sounded like a gull gargling gravel, but he could make out the words.

"That's me. Who's this?"

2

"Not important," the gravel filtered, the words tumbling through the speaker like water over pebbles. "You are the treasure hunter, yes?"

"Yes."

"You know of Cthulhu, of the Great Elder Ones?"

"I do."

"He is coming to earth, on a vacation."

"To earth?"

"Delaware, to be exact." The voice was clearer. Still deep, still fractured, but the longer whoever it was talked, the better they seemed to get at enunciation.

"Is—does he have treasure there?"

"I cannot say."

"When?"

"Two days."

Kansas looked back at the balding man. Two days. Two days and he needed to be in Delaware. It was better than crushing cans from twenty feet away with a whip.

"Thanks."

"I will meet you. Delaware Bay."

"How will I know you?"

"You just will."

"We split the treasure, I suppose?"

"No. You can have any treasure we find. I only want Cthulhu."

"Okay. What's your name?"

3

But the line was dead. The screen on his phone was blank.

"Hey Colin?" Kansas said walking back to his now ex-employer. "That call was an emergency. I have to go away for a couple of weeks."

"A couple weeks? But I was going to print posters."

"I'll call you when I get back."

"Where are you going?"

"Delaware."

Colin smiled. "Delaware? I hear it is very nice this time of year."

Kansas headed for his truck with a wave. He'd need to make a stop for his gear, but everything should be ready to go.

This time, Cthulhu wouldn't escape him without giving up his treasure. Not after the embarrassment of their last encounter.

His balls hurt just thinking about it.

It was a perfect time for revenge.

***

Delaware, Earth, 2023

There were two ways Cthulhu could interact with the humans. The first was to do his best imitation of Delaware Bay, and rise up out of the sea as a giant creature and swallow ships whole. While seamen were delicious, he decided instead to go as "cute Cthulhu." He shrunk himself to slightly larger than the average human and took his familiar humanoid form. He would have to find clothes—the last ones he had from his visit to earth were out of fashion and frankly a little tight even when he sucked in his belly.

But he did have his swimming trunks, the ones he'd been wearing when his sister found him. Since the portal deposited him in the ocean just off the coast, he surfaced to see the area around him.

Gah. The air smelled awful. Flowers were in bloom somewhere, and a salt-water breeze filled his nostrils with the scents of the sea. Sickening. Except for the underlying smell of decaying fish, which he found delightful.

He dove below the waves to find its source and consume it. After he had his fill of sea bass, one of which had been seemingly tangled in some sort of line dragging him toward the shore, he swam toward a tall, cylindrical building.

Memories flooded back of a ship, tossed in the waves and struggling to reach shore. He'd been lazy that night, waited for it to founder on the rocks, and then he'd consumed the occupants.

Fear changed the taste of humans. They almost tasted like smoked chicken, which please him. He'd given up smoking years ago. It was a nice effect, one that produced even more fear in the humans, but it was supposedly bad for you. Still, there were times when he missed it.

The building was called a lighthouse, he remembered. A building designed to warn sailors away from dangerous sections of shoreline.

Danger be damned, it was a perfect place to land. Odd horse-less carriages sat behind the lighthouse, waiting for their little masters to emerge. Ha! Perhaps there was a large human operating one of them, and he could steal his clothing. If not, he'd have to endure the masses at one of their horrible stores. He'd found a place on the internet where odd people often shopped, and although people made fun of them sometimes, he thought he might fit right in among the "People of Walmart" as they were called.

All this raced through his head as he approached the building. He awaited the first human who recognized him, the Evil One who they sought to rule over them.

President.

It had a nice ring to it.

But the building he lived in? Who wanted to rule from a place called the White House? He would need to change that right away.

He heard voices as he approached the building and saw two of the humans talking.

The first was a very thin man. Cthulhu wondered how he managed an existence on this hostile world. He wore a thin, black device around his neck, too, one that was supposed to be decorative but simply looked like a ships propeller about to chop into his neck should someone start the motor.

He also had four eyes, and a bit of patchy hair on his face. Even as humans went, he was especially ugly.

"Ma'am," he said. "We do not offer refunds after the tour is over. I'm sorry about all the stairs, but this is a lighthouse." The thin man sounded like he spoke through his nose and that someone had kicked him somewhere personal recently.

"Well, I thought you would at least have an elevator," the other human, a female, said. He could only see her from the back, but she had broad shoulders and clothing that seemed to accentuate them. Her waist was not too thin, like some human women, and she had curves.

Dreadful looking curves. She wore a short skirt, but her legs were short anyway, and on her feet she wore too-thin shoes with spiked heels he'd never seen before. But they looked like they could hurt someone. Stab them. Her voice was deeper than the male of the species, with a hint of roughness and anger.

"I thought I was speaking to the manager," she said. "Someone who cared about customer service and could help me. Apparently not. Is there anyone else I can talk to about this? Your supervisor, perhaps?"

"No, Karen. I'm the manager and the owner, and I am truly sorry."

"Well, I'm going to note this on my Yelp and Google reviews," she said. "You're going to be sorry."

"Mmmmm," the sound escaped Cthulhu's mouth before he could stop it, and he stood stock still. She turned.

The woman, Karen, wore large, dark coverings over her eyes, so he couldn't see them, but he could feel her piercing stare. He could almost taste her anger from here.

"What are you looking at?" she said, moving her head to look him up and down.

"I—um," Cthulhu struggled for something evil to say, but came up with nothing.

"What is your name?" she asked. It was odd, but there seemed to be a seductive tone under her words.

She was even more disgusting from this angle. Her haircut was half blonde, half dark, and the dark half was cut short, almost down to her skull. The blonde half was long, and she wore dangling metal things from her ears which looked like the long devices used to lure fish.

He hated them. He wanted to spend more time with her, get to know her and her apparent hatred.

"C-c-c-thulhu," he stammered.

"Well, K-k-k-k-k-thulhu," she said, clicking her tongue with every kch sound. "Don't you have a shirt?"

"Well, no. I was hoping—"

"I'm sure the manager won't let you in here without a shirt." Her eyes looked him up and down again. "Or shoes."

"Oh, I don't want—"

"Come with me," she said, offering her hand to shake. "I'm Karen."

"I heard," he said. "I'm Cthulhu." He felt a little drool forming at the corner of his mouth and running down one of the tentacles there.

"There it is," she said. "You're pretty ugly, you know that?"

He just nodded, his tentacles bobbing uncomfortably. He suddenly wished he wasn't quite so ugly.

"Well, you're my kind of ugly," she said. "Come with me."

Just then, Cthulhu heard a long, wailing screech. He turned to look.

A white, pale creature emerged from the waves, struggling to climb onto the rocks.

"Gestalt!" he shouted, hate in his voice. He felt himself getting taller and had to control himself.

Behind him he heard a squeal of tires, and turned to see a large, horseless carriage skidding into the parking lot.

"What is going on?" Karen yelled. There was no fear in her voice, only anger.

Cthulhu felt a warmth rise in him when he looked at her.

"Do you have one of those?" he said, pointing to the truck. A man opened the door and stepped out. Clipped to his belt was a whip, and a brown hat sat cockeyed over his ordinary face.

"Not like that," she said. "I have something better, though. Who is that?"

"That is Kansas Smith. And that creature is Gestalt. They're after me."

"After you? Whatever for?" He felt her hand slip around his forearm and slide up to his solid biceps.

Cthulhu shuddered.

"Different reasons. I'm hungry. I need to get some clothes and something to eat, and to get away from them."

"No problem," she said. "Let's go."

She led him to a horseless carriage. It was white, and huge for just the two of them, with three rows of seats. A plate on the back said Delaware, and under that, in big letters, said "K-Gurl." She got in the driver's seat behind what looked like the wheel that could steer a small ship. He managed to open the large door and get in the other side.

Kansas strode toward them, Gestalt not far behind.

"Hang on," she said. The motor started with a roar, and Cthulhu was thrown back into his seat as she sped around the man and the hideous creature, squealing out onto a stretch of smooth land. A road, he remembered now.

"Can we go to Walmart?" he asked.

She snorted. "No way. You deserve better than that. We're going to the Off-Target outlet."

He'd never heard of the place, but Cthulhu nodded.

He put himself in this woman's hands, admiring her strength and hostility. She'd make a great partner for this vacation.

TWO

Off-Target

K ansas Smith spotted Cthulhu right away. He was shorter than last time he had seen him, but he assumed that was a disguise. Same green skin, webbed hands, strong arms, and those feet.

His balls hurt at the memory under the cup he was wearing as he spun into the parking lot.

Not this time, he thought. *No way.*

The monster was with a woman. She wore large, dark sunglasses, a short skirt tugged down over thick legs, and she looked built for war. Or perhaps to survive a famine.

Was that one of the Great Old Ones in disguise? It couldn't be.

Then he saw another creature and knew this was who he was here to meet. He'd never seen anyone or anything that pale, and it lurched as if unused to gravity and the rough ground of the rocks near the shoreline.

As he screeched to a halt, the beast emerged from the rocks and reached the pavement, where it seemed to be having an easier time.

Kansas threw open the driver's door of his lifted Ford. He slid to the ground and made eye contact. Cthulhu stared, and seemed to swell slightly. Kansas glanced at the new arrival, then back at his quarry and the woman.

They were running toward a large Escalade. The plate read "K-Gurl". The slid inside, the engine roared to life, and they spun out of the parking lot onto the road.

Kansas thought of pursuing them, but his contact was close, but not close enough to get in the truck in time. Besides, a thin man stood looking after Karen and then at each of them.

"He is not coming inside," the thin man said nervously, pointing at the white creature.

"We don't need to come inside," Kansas told him. "We just have a few questions about the two who just left."

As he finished the sentence, the pale creature reached his side. His breath came in ragged gasps, and Kansas understood that whoever or whatever it was, this world was not familiar to it at all.

"Play along," he murmured.

The creature looked puzzled, if that was possible, but remained quiet.

"Kansas. Kansas Smith," he introduced himself. "And you are?"

"Mark. The owner and manager of this lighthouse."

"Pleased to meet you," he said, holding out his hand. The smaller man shook it, and Kansas almost thought he would accidentally crush his thin fingers. Mark's hand was weak, limp, and small.

"Likewise. What is going on here?" his eyes, behind dark rimmed thick glasses, darted too the pale creature.

"We'd like to know the same thing. What can you tell us about the pair who just left?"

"Well, they didn't arrive together, that's for sure. The woman, her name is Karen, took the tour then wanted a refund because of all the stairs, and no elevator."

"She thought there would be an elevator?" Kansas asked.

"Actually, I think she knew there wouldn't be. She just wanted to cause trouble."

"I see." The pale creature beside Kansas remained silent but pointed to a camera above the door. "Does that work?"

Mark nodded, and the two men followed him inside, where he showed them into a security room, more like a closet.

"That vanity plate. Can you believe it?" Kansas turned to look at the creature who had joined him. They were standing in front of a monitor showing the replay of the video feed.

The thin white creature who'd claimed out of the rocks stood next to him in silence. A spider crawled from his eye socket, over his bald head, and then into his ear.

Kansas shuddered. Gross.

"So, where do you think he will go?"

"Northmasshy," the word came out like slush from a Vermont snowblower in springtime. A long, thin tongue emerged from the mouth of the beast, ran over its lips, and then it tried speaking again.

"Normally," it said, the words much clearer, although the tone of its voice reminded Kansas of nails on a chalkboard. "He would go straight to one of his hiding spots to get some spending money. Howetheeer—"

The slur was followed by another run of the tongue, almost serpentine in nature, over the lips again.

Kansas just watched and smiled. He twirled his hand though, as if to say, "Go on, go on."

"However," the creature continued. "With this new woman in tow, who knows."

"Well, it seems we want the same things. I'm Kansas." He held out his hand to shake.

"Gestalt," the creature took his outstretched hand.

Gestalt's skin was…well, clammy would be a compliment. A raw fish, but one that had been sitting a few days and started to rot, would feel like the creature's hand. *His hand,* Kansas corrected himself. There was nothing to indicate the sex of the—well, monster was the best word, so he'd call it a male for now.

He thought he felt bones through the skin during that brief contact, but somehow they felt softer than normal bones. The creature had some kind of muscle tone, but it looked like certain muscles had been misplaced. Gestalt's biceps hung to low on his upper arm. Shoulder muscles, though lean, were bunched up by his neck on both sides.

His grip was firm, but not strong, even though his forearms bulged oddly near the elbow.

"It" wasn't human. It was something humanoid, and Kansas suspected this was not its true form any more than the walking, humanoid Cthulhu was in his true form either.

Armed with the plate number and a general direction the pair were headed, Kansas turned to the manager, Mark.

"I think this is all we need, but can we call you if we need more?"

"Sure," Mark told them. "Here's my card."

"WHOA THERE!" A redshirted individual stopped Cthulhu as they approached the front doors. "You got a shirt, buddy?"

He pointed to a sign with some symbols, and to his surprise, Cthulhu was able to easily decipher them. His talent for language was coming in handier than that time with the wooden horse in Mesopotamia. Or was it Turkey? No matter.

"No shirt, no service," it read.

Service? He wasn't entirely familiar with the concept. Just as he was about to turn to Karen and ask her to act as his service so he wouldn't need a shirt, she stepped in front of him.

"Excuse me?" she said. "We lost our things on the beach, and I need to buy my boyfriend—" At that word she pulled him forward locking her arm in his. He moved next to her and tried to smile. As he did, the redshirt looked away and grimaced.

"—my boyfriend," Karen continued, "a new shirt and some more clothes for the rest of our trip."

Cthulhu saw the man with the red shirt step back. The symbols on a round device attached to his clothing somehow read, "Tucker."

Good thing no one misspelled that name, he thought. Out loud, he laughed, a sound more like a dying seagull gargling blood, and Tucker took another step back.

"I can't—I mean, I am just—" he stammered and stopped.

Karen lowered the round things covering her eyes by sliding them down her nose and looked over them. "Are you saying I may need to speak to——" She stopped and raised her neatly plucked eyebrows.

"A m-m-m-m-manager?" he managed.

"Well?"

Tucker had clearly encountered Karen or someone much like her before, because his shoulders sagged, and he turned to one side, gesturing toward the door with an outstretched arm.

"Go ahead," he said. "But grab a shirt, rip the tags off to pay at the register, and put it on. Maybe some shoes too," he said, pointing at Cthulhu's feet. "Otherwise, if the manager does see you, she might have my head."

"She?" Karen said with an undertone of joy in her voice. Cthulhu recognized it clearly. She was spoiling for a fight and knew another woman would be much better competition than the weak males of the species he'd seen so far.

He laughed again, and that did it. The employee stepped back. Cthulhu smiled as the doors opened automatically as they approached and slid shut after they passed through. Cool air hit his skin, almost tickling him.

"Did you see him jump?" Karen said as they walked in. "That was great. What was that sound you made?"

"I was laughing," Cthulhu said.

"That is how you laugh?"

He nodded his face getting hot behind his tentacles. He didn't recognize the feeling at first. Embarrassment? Was that what he was feeling?

He found himself wanting to impress Karen, and almost fearing he wasn't doing a good job.

Fear? The ultimate evil? Afraid? Impossible!

Yet it seemed it was so, and he waited as she studied him. Then she laughed too, a loud sound punctuated with snorts, and he smiled. They were not so different after all.

"Let's go," she said. "Hopefully they have something in this horrible place that will fit you and not cost an arm and a leg."

Cthulhu hoped so too. He only had two arms and legs in this form, and it would take him time to grow each back. His vacation, if it could be called that now that he was being chased, could only last a week, two at the outside. Like it or not, he still had a job among the Great Old Ones, and his PTO was limited. The job conditions were horrible, and the benefits sucked, just the way he liked it. Working for El-Moron was almost like free torture.

He didn't even want to be gone long. But all torture and no play made Jack a dull, dull boy.

They headed for a large sign that said "Menswear" in large white letters.

The first rack they came to had a sign that read, "Buy One Get One FREE."

No mention of arms or legs.

Karen looked at him, and said, "Double X will have to do for you, I hope."

A section of the rack had a little circle that had two X's and one L, and he assumed that was the section he should look in. He reached out a hand and started to flip through the shirts one at a time.

"Excuse me," a voice came from behind them. The voice was feminine, but deep and laced with authority. Cthulhu glanced that way, but saw Karen already turning to handle the situation.

He was cold, so wanted to find at least a shirt fairly quickly. He had no idea how he would pay for things. He had a pouch of gold coins on his belt but hadn't really thought about what money they would be using in this time and place.

Perhaps Karen could help. He could trade her for some local currency.

Behind him, he heard her say, "Can I help you?"

"Yeah. I'm the manager, Ellen. Your friend needs a shirt, shoes, and maybe a little deodorant or a toothbrush to be in here."

"Are you insulting my boyfriend?"

The word amused Cthulhu, and he laughed. A tiny, fish laden belch followed, and he smiled. "Excuse me," he said.

"Definitely a toothbrush," the manager said.

"Listen, we lost our stuff on the beach, and we're here to grab a few things."

"He needs a shirt."

"We're buying him a shirt."

Then Cthulhu saw it and threw his head back, roaring with joy. "This one! This is my shirt!"

Sure enough, like the meme on social media, he was holding a shirt with his likeness on the front, albeit a little blue to match the shirt background.

"Cthulhu for President" it said. Underneath in smaller letters, it said, "Why Choose the Lesser Evil?"

"It is mine! All mine!" he shouted.

Karen smiled. "You see? My boyfriend is a celebrity." She took the shirt from his hands and ripped the price tag off. "Here, put it on."

Cthulhu did, stretching it a little to go over his head, and pulling it down. It was a little tight, so he thought really hard, changing his form slightly. It fit perfectly.

He smiled and struck a pose, one like he'd seen people selling clothes online do.

Karen giggled and clapped her hands. "See, Ellen, shirt. We will go get him some shoes next. Can you take these—" she handed the manager the tags she'd removed from the shirt. "—up front to the register and keep them for us. We'll be there in a few moments."

Ellen scurried off, they headed for the shoe department. Cthulhu skipped along the way. It had been a long time since he had anything he could call fun.

Things had never felt this way with Idh-yaa. His former embarrassment was gone, and he and Karen chatted as they looked for sneakers that would fit his giant, webbed feet.

They laughed and joked as he tried some on, a few he couldn't even get over his webbed toes.

Cthulhu heard a sound from behind him, like a human clearing their throat, and he turned to look.

A man stood there wearing what kind of looked like a military uniform, with a shiny symbol on his chest. On the other side was a name of some sort. There were a lot of letters, and

Cthulhu had no idea how to pronounce STRADI-VARINISKI all pressed together like that.

Karen turned too, and even she looked nervous.

"You're going to have to leave now, sir," he said.

Cthulhu stood there, a sneaker hanging dangling from one hand by the shoelaces and did the only thing he could think of.

He roared.

His tentacles blew outward with a rush of sound, air, and foul air drawn from the depths of his generous lungs.

STRADIVRINISKI fell backward, tripping and falling into the racks of clothing behind him.

"That was amazing!" Karen said. "But we better go, before he calls for backup."

Cthulhu took the shoes he had been trying on, and they ran toward the front of the store.

A crowd ran ahead of them, and a couple of times Cthulhu glanced back to see what they were running from but saw nothing. They just moved with the crowd. One man tripped and fell in front of him, and Cthulhu stepped over him with a roar.

"Watch where you're going!"

The crowd scattered once outside, and Karen and Cthulhu walked to her waiting horseless carriage, and no one tried to stop them.

"Where to next?" Karen asked.

Cthulhu had no idea.

THREE

Evil Minds and Motorola

K ansas would have been concerned about his upholstery, if it was anything to be concerned about. But it was not. In fact, it was a disaster of sorts, and he'd never been so grateful for the tattered passenger seat and worn headrest.

His primary concern was the spiders. He wanted to say something helpful, like, "Dude, there's a spider on your earlobe building a web to your nose." But whenever he opened his mouth to say anything, he just had no idea how to say it.

So he stayed silent as the creature—he—Gestalt, he tried to correct himself. The creature had a name.

"So, Gestalt, where are you from?"

The question felt stupid as he said it, but how could he make conversation with—well, this?

A large slurping sound followed. "I'm from the same place as Cthulhu, the Land of the Great Old Ones."

"Are you one of the Great Old Ones?" Kansas glanced over as he started the truck and saw a blush of pink on Gestalt's pale cheeks. Embarrassment?

"How nice of you to think so. No, I serve the Great Old One, Elhort. He is my…master."

"Your master?"

"I am here at his command. Who is your master?"

"Well, I don't have a—I am my own master."

"So you are one of the Great Old Ones of this world?"

"Well, I'm not old."

"I meant no disrespect, oh Great One."

"I also have no idea how great I am."

"Whoever is his own master is a Great One. I serve Elhort, but I will also serve you in this quest."

"Serve me? No, you don't—"

"Allow me to do this thing. It will be my honor."

"Um, okay. But you can just be my partner. There is no serving necessary."

Gestalt grabbed his wrist. "I must serve you, Great One. Do not deny me this."

"I—

But just as he spoke, a crackle came from a speaker on the dashboard, followed by a beep.

"K.S., you got your ears on?"

Kansas reached for and picked up a mic with a corded cable, attached to a ham radio on the dash.

"Yeah, go ahead, over." His radio protocol was shit, but he checked to make sure they were on the secure channel he would set up. Any ham operator just surfing would never find it.

"You got a police scanner? You're up in Delaware right, looking for that Cthulhu thing, over?"

"Yes, sir."

"Well, you should turn on your radio or scanner. Something just happened at an Off-Target outlet you should know about."

"Thanks for the tip. I'll check it out. Over." He added the last word, even though he knew he didn't need to.

"You bet. Out."

Kansas fiddled with his phone. You could have an old fashioned police scanner, but like everything else, there was an app for that.

"Seven-five-niner," a voice came through as soon as launched the app and connected the speaker to the Bluetooth speaker on the dash. "We're looking for a white Escalade, 2019, vanity plate K-Gurl. Headed northwest, two occupants, one male, one female. One suspect considered dangerous, even though he's unarmed."

"Were there any injuries at the scene?"

"Negative central. Quite a few folks scared, and one man injured himself fleeing, but the man in question stepped over him."

"Description of the suspects?"

"White female, haircut half-blonde, half dark-haired, large sunglasses, five-five, and around 175. Male subject, six foot four or so, accounts vary, green skinned, facial deformity. One witness described him as a tentacle face, whatever that means."

"Okay, we'll get a chopper in the air."

The truck was already in gear and Kansas was rolling, headed out of the parking lot and on to the road.

Gestalt slid around on the seat, figured out how to fasten his seat belt, and then looked over at Kansas. A slurping sound was followed by words.

"I'm hungry. Can we get a thing called a haammff…" Gravel gargle. "A hamburger?"

"Sure," Kansas said. They won't get far. He turned on the ham radio again. "We'll hit a drive through."

As much as the slimy face could hold an expression, Gestalt looked both puzzled and pleased.

"K.S. here," Kansas said after keying the mic. "I need some directions and some eyes. Anyone out there, over?"

"What's the cut for assistance?" A female voice came back. He gulped. The Black Widow. She'd love Gestalt and everything about him.

"Ten percent," Kansas said.

"Twelve and you got a deal. Over."

It took Kansas only a second to answer. This was the chance of a lifetime. He knew it was going to cost him.

"Deal," he answered.

"Okay, what's your 20?"

Kansas told her where they were, and about where they were headed.

"See you in an hour. Out."

He felt better already. He changed apps on the phone and searched burger joints near me. He wondered if Gestalt had any treasure of his own. This trip was about to get expensive.

CTHULHU'S STOMACH GROWLED LOUDLY. He was hungry. Keeping this form was hard work, and the only food he'd eaten was the fish he'd managed to grab from the waves on the swim into shore.

He was thirsty too, and he glanced over at Karen who looked him up and down. He was now dressed in what appeared to be oversized sneakers, swim trunks, and a Cthulhu for President shirt that just barely fit.

She smiled and reached for his hand. He let her take it.

"Are you hungry?" she asked gently.

"I am," he said. "Thirsty, too."

"Well, let's get you some food, shall we? What would you like?"

"Fish," he said without thinking.

"That we can do. Fish and chips coming up. We also need to talk about getting rid of this car, at least temporarily. The police will be looking for it after our little stunt at Off-Target. Do you have any money?"

Cthulhu took the leather pouch from his swim trunks pocket and handed it over. "Only this," he said. "I was hoping to trade."

Karen's eyes went wide, nearly eclipsing her overly large sunglasses as the weight of the bag landed in her hand.

She opened it and her mouth opened wide, too. Her lips moved, like she was trying to speak, and for a moment Cthulhu thought she might be hurt or need some help or something.

Then she managed to make words. "Is this gold?"

"Yes. I can get more, if we need it," he told her. "I have treasure stashed all kinds of place on Earth, including close to here."

"Oh, I think this will do nicely," she said. "Let's get something to eat and then we will go to a coin dealer I know. He will trade us some cash for one or two of these. You can keep the rest for later."

"You can have those," Cthulhu told her. "I have lots more where that came from."

"You do?"

"That's why Kansas Smith is after me. He's a treasure hunter."

"And the pale guy?"

"That's Gestalt. He wants to return me home. Elhort, one of the Great Old Ones, was not in favor of me coming here. Gestalt is his servant."

"His servant? How awful."

"Hey, it's not as bad as it seems. He could have been married to my ex-wife."

"You have an ex-wife?"

"Long story, but yes."

"I see." Karen got quiet, and Cthulhu worried again for a moment, until she pulled into the parking lot of a restaurant. "Let's get some food first of all, and then we can move on."

She parked and they went inside. The clerk looked oddly at Cthulhu, but the smell of fish in the place overwhelmed him. He literally wined before Karen shushed him.

She ordered three orders of "Fish and Chips." The chips were wedged and fried potatoes of some sort, and they smelled heavenly too.

The cashier gave them a little triangle number, and Karen even bought him a baseball cap that read, "Cal's Seafood."

"You didn't have to do that," he said as she placed it gently on his head.

"Well, it's a good way to help disguise you, and besides, it looks cute on you."

Cthulhu blushed. "Thanks."

"So your ex. Tell me more."

"We were married for years. Four kids. But when they went off to their own lives, we grew apart."

"And?"

"And everything I did tended to irritate her, or so it seemed. I got a little—feisty about it, and then was the straw that broke the camel's back so to speak."

"That was?"

"Leaving the toilet seat up. I really had been doing better, but she made me so mad, so I left it up on purpose. It—didn't end well."

"I would imagine not. Was she pretty?"

Cthulhu thought that through. If he said yes, it wouldn't be exactly true. If he said no, Karen might think he was mean.

"She was pretty enough. We did love each other, once. But that love just faded over time. It really is too bad." He tried to look sad, but he wasn't really. He was happy Idh-yaa had left him. He was happy to be single, here with this wonderfully hateful and angsty woman who seemed to adore him.

"Well, I am not in favor of divorce," she said. "I have been divorced. Twice. But that does not mean I like it or intend to get divorced again. You understand?"

He did. If he pursued anything with Karen, it would have to involve commitment.

That didn't scare him, but it did make him uncomfortable.

They were interrupted by their food arriving.

Cthulhu could not stop himself. He grabbed a slab of fish, stuffed it past his tentacles into his mouth, and slurped a bit of the tartar sauce to chase it down. He reached for another as he saw Karen delicately nibbling on a battered filet. He stopped, swallowed, and resolved to slow down.

So he stuffed three of the "chips" into his mouth rather than the five he thought he could fit. Karen took a couple more bites and then smiled at him. She laughed as he tore a second filet in half and tried to delicately bite a piece from it. The act frustrated him, and he shoved the whole bit into his mouth.

"Just eat," she said. "Like you normally would. I want you to be yourself."

He finished the first and second baskets of fish and chips, in short order. Karen had half a filet left and slid it his way. He finished in one bite, and then tried to wipe his tentacles with the provided napkins, with minimal success.

He then slurped a sweet beverage called "Coke" from a straw shoved into a giant cup. It tasted so good, he nearly finished it in one slurp.

Karen smiled again. "Let me get you some more. Do you want a milkshake?"

Cthulhu was not sure what that was, but it sounded interesting, so he nodded.

Karen returned to the table with more Coke and a thick liquid. He took a drink and loved the taste. But he stopped himself. He slid the icy cup over to Karen.

She took a sip and licked her lips. The very act made him feel warm all over.

"That is so good," she said. "Let's take it with us and head for the coin dealer."

"You bet," he said. They headed for the car, the Coke in his hand, and Karen carrying the shake.

Once they got inside, she leaned over and pressed her lips to his cheek.

"What was that for?" he asked.

"I like you. Thanks for being honest about your wife."

"Sure, I guess," he said. "You're welcome?"

"I needed to know you were someone I could trust."

Cthulhu did not know what to say, so he put his hand out. She took it, and they looked into each other's eyes.

Just then a police car turned into the parking lot. The officer stopped, looked at Karen's horseless carriage, and Cthulhu could see him talking into something.

"We've been spotted," Karen said. "Let's get out of here."

She started the vehicle and shifted something. A short chirp of a siren sounded from the police vehicle.

"Hang on!" she said, releasing Cthulhu's hand, and he felt the large vehicle bump over the curb in front of them. They sped across the parking lot and squealed out onto the street.

He looked back, and the law officer was nowhere to be found.

FOUR

Somebody's Watching You

The inside of Kansas' truck was a mess. Gestalt was naturally a messy person just due to his—well, person. The spiders had stopped crawling, thankfully. But he seemed to leave an oily-slime on every surface he sat on or touched.

When he ate, he seemed to miss his mouth more often than not. It was clear he felt awkward in this form, and Kansas idly wondered what he really looked like, and then regretted every image his mind put up.

French fry pieces, bits of hamburger, spots of ketchup, and used napkins, some that looked as if the corners had been chewed off of them dotted the passenger side dash, the door on that side, and even the window.

Gestalt belched, and a foul odor filled the truck interior. Damn. Gross.

"Are you done?" Kansas asked. He'd eaten one burger himself, and a medium fry. His companion had consumed three, and what seemed like a five pound bag of fried spuds. Forty bucks was a little much to spend for two people at a burger joint.

This better pay off big.

As Gestalt attempted to slurp the last of a milkshake through a straw, Kansas drank the last of his Dr. Pepper, and then rolled his window down. The radio crackled to life.

"Black Widow," the voice said. "That you in the blue truck? Over."

"Yeah. Where are you?"

A second later a black, lifted Ford appeared in front of them, and Kansas smiled. It felt like things were going to be okay now.

A slim and rather short woman slipped from the truck. He could see that she was armed, a too-large for her frame pistol strapped to her belt. He would have to dial her back a little bit on that.

She came over to the truck, and then jumped back. The pistol appeared in her hand, and Kansas was impressed by how steady it was.

"Whoa! What is that?"

"This is Gestalt. He's... um, helping?"

"I mean, what is he?"

"Well, he's an emissary from the Elder Ones. He's here to return Cthulhu to his rightful place among them. Did I get that right?"

A giant slurp came from Gestalt, and the Black Widow recoiled. By now, Kansas knew he was simply preparing to speak.

"That is correct," he said. "Does this woman wish to play a part in our quest?"

"She will help me, yes, in return for part of the treasure we find, if we find it."

Gestalt seemed to grin. "Do you need money? To help with this quest?"

Kansas looked at the new arrival, and she nodded, but only slightly. She never took her eyes off of Gestalt, and her skin had gone pale, causing her red lips to stand out from her sharp and angular features. She ran her tongue over them.

Kansas turned back in time to see Gestalt reach what seemed like literally into his skin on his stomach. The result was an odd squishing sound, and then he withdrew a leather pouch. It dripped with some kind of clear slime for a moment, but once a few strands of it dropped onto the already stained upholstery, it seemed to dry. The creature worked it open by untangling the strings securing the top with his slim fingers. Tipping it up, he dropped two gold coins into his palm.

"Issshhh—" Gravel sounds were followed by another slurp. "Is there a place we can exchange this for your money?"

Kansas held out his hand, and the creature dropped the two coins into his palm. He hefted them, figuring them at about an ounce each.

He turned to see Black Widow's back to him. She was bent over, and a puddle of whatever she had eaten lately lay in the parking lot at her feet.

"You okay?" he asked.

She turned around, wiping her mouth with her sleeve. "Yeah, yeah. Just—that thing—eww."

"I get it, but I have something that might help you get past his appearance."

"What might that be?"

Kansas held out the gold coins. "Know anywhere we could get some cash for these?"

She plucked one from his palm and stared at it. "Is this real?"

"I have no reason to believe it is not."

Another slurp altered him another speech was coming. "They are solid gold. As solid as the Elder Ones can refine it. I understand that metal has value in your world?"

"It does. Does Cthulhu carry these as well?"

"He is much wealthier than I. Elhort gave me some funding for the trip to return him."

"Do you have more?" the Black Widow blurted out.

"I do," the creature said. The tone of his voice dropped to one much deeper, a voice laced with hatred.

This. This was much closer to his real voice and his real form, Kansas thought.

"I will share all of it with you if we find him, and if we do it quickly."

Kansas stared at him and managed to nod.

"Do you require nourishment?" Gestalt addressed the Black Widow for the first time.

"W-w-w-hat?" she asked. It seemed impossible, or at least improbable that her face could have gotten any paler without being transparent. She nearly appeared to be a relative of the creature who'd joined them, and now seemed to be directing them in some ways.

"Do you need nourishment?" he repeated. "Food. A—" he hesitated. "A hamburger or French fries?"

"No. I'm good," she said.

"Then let us go get the funds you need and get on with our journey."

Kansas looked up from tapping on his phone.

"I know just the place to start. Cthulhu will have to get money, too, right?"

"I imagine so." Black Widow said.

"The woman he is with, she doesn't appear to have been kidnapped. She appears to be with him willingly," Kansas said.

"Right."

"Then she must want something, too. His treasure maybe?"

"Why else would anyone be with such a hideous creature?" Gestalt said.

"Why, indeed?" Kansas answered. "You want to follow us?"

"Where are we going?" Black Widow asked.

"Here," he said, turning the phone toward her. The screen showed a pawn shop not far away.

"Stan's Coin and Gun," the screen read. "Specializing in antique guns and coins."

"Good call," she said. "I'll be right behind you."

With that, she escaped to her truck, glancing back from time to time. Kansas had expected her to be intrigued, not frightened. He'd never seen the ex-soldier and now treasure hunter so freaked out in the entire time he'd known her.

UP AHEAD, Cthulhu saw a sign.

"Stan's Coin and Gun" it read. Karen pulled in, and then pulled around back into a parking lot. She backed her large vehicle into a space against the fence and almost around the corner from what appeared to be a back door.

The brick building appeared to have once been a home, but there were bars over every window, and Cthulhu could see at least four locks on the back door.

"He takes security seriously," he said.

"That's okay," Karen said. She grabbed a huge purse with the word "Coach" on a gold plate on the side, and he wondered what kind of coach she was. She didn't look like a sports coach. In fact, quite the opposite unless perhaps she coached weight lifting or something.

No matter. He admired her stocky and muscular form as she slid from the carriage. She turned to look back at him.

"Well, are you coming?" she asked before arming her face with her large sunglasses.

"Yes, yes," he said, opening the door on his side and sliding out.

"Were you staring at me?" she asked when he came around the car.

He stopped, wary of answering. If he said "yes" she might find it creepy. If he said "no" she would likely catch him quickly in the lie. That would not do either.

She made him feel funny, off-kilter and back on his heels. It was not something he was used to at all.

"Yes," he said. "I was admiring the way you look."

"You find me pretty?"

"Gorgeous!" he said before he could stop himself.

"You are a flatterer," she said, but there was a smirk there he kind of loved. He couldn't see her eyes, but he could feel her gaze on him.

Cthulhu blushed and had to look away. As he did, he felt her hand slide around his arm, and then felt her lips touch his cheek.

Warmth raced through him.

"I find you attractive, too," Karen said. "We can talk about that later. For now, let's get inside, get some money, and figure out what to do next.

They walked toward the building, now arm in arm. He looked across the street and saw a lot decorated with streamers and filled with various horseless carriages with numbers on the windshield.

Right up front was a large, green vehicle. It looked military in origin, with large, knobby tires, a thin, but wide profile, and an armored appearance.

"Rare Hummer!" The text on the front windshield said.

"Can we get that?" he asked her.

"That's a bit conspicuous, but we will see," she said. "Let's see how much we can get for a few of your coins."

They hit a buzzer beside the door, and it clicked open. The pair stepped inside, and then the outer door closed behind them before the inner door opened.

It reminded Cthulhu of an airlock, something he had seen on space ships he'd attacked from time to time while crossing the galaxy.

They walked inside to find a man with gold rimmed spectacles looking at them. His hand was right next to a large pistol on the counter.

"What do you want?" he asked.

"Well, that isn't the kind of customer service I would expect for someone entering your shop," Karen said. "Are you the manager?"

"Owner, manager, sole proprietor, and pretty damn good with his here gun. Who's the big fella with you?"

"I'm Karen, and this is Cthulhu," she said. "We have something to sell, but if you are not interested, we can take it elsewhere."

"Let me see it."

"You should change the way you are talking to me," Karen said. "Or my online review of your business might reflect your rudeness."

"Let me see it, please," Stan said.

Karen elbowed Cthulhu in the ribs, and he removed the pouch from the pocket of his swim trunks. He moved to hand it to the shop owner, but Karen stopped him. She took the pouch, opened it, and dropped a single coin in her hand, clearly showing Stan there were others.

The man's eyes widened, and he pushed up his glasses with the hand that had been next to the pistol. His hand opened and closed in a "gimme" gesture.

"We want your best offer," Karen said. "We know what these coins are worth, and if you mess with us, we will go somewhere else."

Cthulhu wanted to protest. They needed money, and even if this man lowballed them on value, they could just sell him a couple of them, and sell more later, elsewhere.

But Karen was clearly the expert in this area, in this world. He could see other coins, some that even interested the treasure hoarder in him, under the glass in this shop.

He could have forced the owner to give them all to him. But he didn't want to do that. It might draw unwanted attention. He wanted to get somewhere where he could relax and enjoy himself, without running, even for a few days.

He grunted instead, swallowing the roar he had ready, and pasted his best smile on his face.

The shop owner barely looked at him. He took the coin gently in his hand, and then pulled a loupe hanging on a lanyard around his neck up to his eye. He studied it for a second.

"Spanish in origin. Ancient. Fantastic condition, although some wear marks from being in the pouch, obviously. Not machined. This is the real deal."

He looked up and Karen smiled at him. Cthulhu remained silent, remembering the ship the coins had come from and how good it had felt to rip it in half and send it to the bottom of the sea. There was still treasure on that ship: he'd only taken about half of it, and this little pouch was a fraction of what he had stored—well, somewhere in what was now Connecticut, he thought to himself.

Stan brought out a scale and weighed the coin carefully. "Thirty and a half grams," he said in awe. "Just over an ounce. May I see another?"

His originally harsh demeanor had softened.

Out the window, Cthulhu saw a police vehicle drive slowly by followed by another going the opposite direction.

He tapped Karen on the shoulder.

"I see them," she hissed. "We have a few more minutes. Relax, and let me do the talking."

"Sure," she told Stan. "What do you think they are worth?"

"Well, how much are you looking for?" he asked. "And where did you get these?" He looked at the second coin, and returned to muttering, not that interested in her answer, at least not yet.

"Just as pristine as the first," he said. "Fabulous."

"What will you give me for them?"

"How many do you have?"

"Enough. How much?"

Stan sucked air through his teeth, and Cthulhu watched him carefully, ready to spring if he tried anything stupid.

"Well, the gold alone is worth just under $2 grand," he said. "But the historical value—"

"Yes?"

"I would love to have five of these. Thing is, I don't know if I have enough cash to give you what these are really worth. But we can make a trade if you like. Do you—need anything?" Stan gestured around his shop.

"Well, we do need a car. We are having some trouble with ours," Karen said. "And then we'll take cash for the rest."

"I just happen to own the lot across the street," he said. "What are you looking for?"

"That one," Cthulhu said, pointing at the Rare Hummer. "Full of fuel."

"Oh, that's a beaut, but it's worth—"

"Worth less than five coins. How much cash do you have, Stan?"

He looked at her, and then looked at Cthulhu, seeming to really see him for the first time.

"Hey, you're—nice shirt," he said. "How about the Hummer and five grand for five coins."

"Deal," Karen told hm. "And hurry up. We're late for an appointment."

Stan rushed through the paperwork, which Karen quickly signed. Another police car passed by, slowly, and then continued on.

They took the keys from Stan, then made their way again through the security doors. They stopped at Karen's vehicle, and Cthulhu graciously dragged her large suitcase behind him and across the street.

They ran across the street after waiting for traffic to clear. Karen went to the driver's door of the large vehicle, but Cthulhu stopped her.

"I would like to drive," he said.

"You would like to drive?"

"Yes."

"Do you know how?" she asked, looking him up and down.

"I know the basics," he said. "And I am sure you would be a wonderful teacher."

It was the flattery that got her, he was sure. Cthulhu slid behind the wheel, thinking back to all the things he'd seen Karen doing, and the limited driving he'd done before on earth.

That had involved a lot of crashing, something he wanted to avoid this time.

He inserted the key, fired up the motor, and pulled forward, over the parking barrier and the sidewalk, onto the street.

The obstacles hardly jolted the rugged vehicle.

"Whoo hoo!" he said. He glanced over to see Karen smiling.

"Whoop!" she said. "This thing is great."

"Where to?" he asked.

"Let's get out of this town before we get caught," she said. "There's a Marriot a couple towns over, and I'm a member of their rewards program."

"Great," he said. He looked in the mirror as they pulled away, and saw a large pickup followed by a second one pulling into the pawn shop parking lot.

He thought he recognized the first one, and maybe the second. They made him feel uncomfortable, and he increased his speed as they drove away.

FIVE

Trading Cars and Places

"That's a nice Hummer, over," Black Widow's voice came over the radio.

"It is," Kansas replied. "Too bad we don't have one of those. How do you want to work the approach?"

He pulled around the back of the pawn shop and spotted a white SUV in the corner of the lot.

"Wait!" he said. "I think that's the Escalade Karen was driving. Approach with caution."

But as soon as the truck rolled to a stop, Gestalt was out the door and sprinting across the lot. The creature moved with more speed and grace than he thought possible, and Kansas followed, drawing a cannister of pepper spray as he ran. The Black Widow, the only name he knew the woman by, was close behind, drawing her weapon.

"No!" he shouted. "We need him alive!"

She lowered the weapon slightly but continued to run, keeping pace with him.

Ahead, Gestalt grabbed the handle on the door of the SUV and yanked, hard. The door did not budge, clearly locked.

He pulled harder, and Kansas saw the odd muscles under his skin tighten and almost normalize for a moment.

The door flew open and then it was in the creature's hand. He tossed it aside like it was cardboard, looked inside the vehicle, and roared.

His eyes glowed red, and he raised his fists in anger, roaring a second time at the sky.

Kansas could guess why, but a second later he looked inside. The vehicle was empty.

"Damn!" he said, looking around. Cthulhu and Karen had gotten here first.

Maybe they were still inside.

The back door of the red-brick building looked armored, and there were no less than four visible locks.

Bars covered all of the windows.

The place looked quiet. He looked at Black Widow, then nodded at the back door. She nodded back, and they moved away.

In a flash, Gestalt was ahead of them. He roared and pulled at the bars. Kansas saw them bend slightly. They held, but the creature *bent* them.

"Stop!" he hissed. "Just stop and listen!"

Gestalt turned, his alien features twisted in anger, his eyes glowing, heat radiating from his body.

A gargle came from his throat.

"Why. Must. We. Wait?" he asked, clearly struggling with each word.

"Because whoever is in there is probably armed, number one. And if Cthulhu and Karen are still there, you just let them know we are here and spooked them."

The odd head cocked. He was listening. Good.

Kansas breathed a sigh and continued. "We need to talk our way into this. Either get to them or find out where they went. If you bull your way in there, we can't do any of that."

"Okay, okay," he said.

The creature backed off, and Kansas stepped forward, the Black Widow close behind. He was glad to see she'd holstered her weapon and at least appeared to be calm.

He pushed the buzzer beside the door, and it opened. He motioned the others to step inside.

They followed, finding another door closed ahead of them.

The outer door closed and locked, and Kansas expected the inner door to open as well.

It did not. Instead, he heard a voice from above.

"What do you want?" It said, crackling through an unseen speaker.

"We have something to sell you," Kansas began.

"I'm not buying the rest of the day," the voice responded. "Come back tomorrow."

Kansas held out a coin, hoping whatever camera was watching them could see it.

"Not even for one of these?"

There was a long pause. Then a buzzer sounded, and the inner door opened. Gestalt started to rush through, but Kansas stopped him with a hand on his slimy arm. He could feel the tension in the creature.

"Stop," he said. "Let me."

"Graaatthhee," Gestalt said, but backed down.

Kansas and Black Widow went inside. A man stood behind the counter, round in body, plump in face, hand near a pistol on a counter.

"Hey, there," Kansas said, but the man stopped him. He tapped the pistol with his forefinger.

"Before you come a step further, I want you to know you are not the first to show up with rare coins today. I want to see what you have first, but I am flat out of cash right now, so even if what you have is great, you'll have to wait for cash."

"What do you mean not the first?" the Black Widow said.

"Odd couple was just in here with a bunch of old Spanish coins. I bought a few but told them to come back later with the rest if they wanted more money. We made a partial trade. Perhaps you would be interested in something similar?"

"We'll see. You want to look at what we have first?" Kansas asked.

The Black Widow looked around at the weapons in the place with obvious hunger. Gestalt stood impatiently.

"Sure," the man said. "I'm Stan by the way."

"Kansas Smith. This is Black Widow, and this is Gestalt."

"What a group," he said with a sigh. "The couple just here were Karen and Cthulhu."

"Really? What did they have?"

"Let me see the coin," Stan said. "They had some Spanish bullion, from a wreck off the US coast I would reckon, but I haven't looked in detail yet. This—this is earlier even. Roman?" he said, looking at Gestalt closely for the first time. His eyes widened, and then Kansas could see his face contort as he tried to control his expression.

He put a loupe to his eye and turned the coin over several times. "Yes, yes. Early, early. I will have to look, but—"

Next to him, on the counter, was a scale. He placed the coin carefully on it. "Twenty-nine grams. Yes, this is wonderful."

"How much?" Kansas asked again.

"Two for just the gold. Seven per coin on the open market. I would give you thirty-five hundred, but as I said, short on cash."

"That's okay," the Black Widow said from a couple aisles over. "We'll take this and come back tomorrow for the cash."

She emerged from the aisle, holding a large, odd looking weapon. In her other hand, she held what appeared to be three large nets with weights on the corners. "This should cost about half of your offer for that coin. Get more cash, and we'll be back with more coins."

"More of these?" Stan said greedily.

"Those and more," she said. "We'll have a whole treasure chest full. And we'll need someone to broker it. Would that be you, Stan?"

He smiled, his puffy cheeks meeting the thin gold rims of his glasses, his clearly polished false teeth gleaming.

"I'm your man," he said. "No question."

"Now, where did the other two go?" Kansas asked.

"Well, I can help you a great deal with that. One of the things they traded me for was a Hummer."

"Military? Great shape?"

"Yep."

"We saw them leaving. Damn. Well, it shouldn't be hard to track."

"Well, not hard at all," Stan said.

"What do you mean?" the Black Widow asked.

"Well, when I bought it at action, it was Lo-Jacked. I repro-grammed the chip."

"And?" Kansas interjected, intrigued.

"And you can track it with this," he said, pulling a device from under the counter.

It showed a map on a small screen, and a little red dot was traveling rapidly along the blue line of a road.

Gestalt stared at it, confused.

"That, and the net gun for the lady in trade for one coin. Bring more tomorrow. Let me know what you have, and I'll set up the buyers for you. For a small commission of course."

"Small commission?" Kansas asked. The Black Widow picked up the device and stared at it, pushing a couple more buttons.

"Ten percent," Stan said. "I'll do all the legwork for you."

"Deal."

They shook hands, and the trio left the building.

"Where to?" Kansas asked.

"Follow me," the Black Widow said. "I think I know where they are going and look." She held out the device, and Kansas looked at the screen.

The red dot that represented the Hummer was stationary. They were stopped.

He smiled. "We got him."

"I have a better idea," the Black Widow said.

She outlined what she wanted to do, and Kansas nodded. Gestalt listened, seeming to understand everything they were talking about.

When she finished speaking, he let out a roar. This time, it was not a cry of rage, but of celebration. They all felt victory was quite close. The treasure, and Cthulhu himself, would soon be in their grasp.

"WOULD you like to go for a swim?" Karen asked.

"Would I?" Cthulhu said. "I would love to!"

If he was honest with himself, and he was brutally so, all this walking around on land was tiresome. He was a sea creature by nature, and the idea of a swim invigorated him.

"Are we going to the ocean?" he asked.

They had checked into the hotel with little trouble. Karen had insisted on and of course received a third-floor room, one with a view, and Cthulhu could see the bay from their window. He flexed and stretched.

"No, we can just use the pool here," Karen told him. "You'll love it, and they have a hot tub. Which reminds me, we need to get you some more clothes. You can't live in those swim trunks, you know."

He did know. He could actually live without clothing at all, but on visits to earth he'd found that to be less than acceptable. In fact, on one trip to Beverly Hills, it had nearly gotten him arrested and then earned him a small roll in a film.

He'd never actually seen it appear in theaters, but he'd been told it was released directly to some kind of streaming platform. The title was "The Fifth Tentacle" or something, and the camera had been at an odd angle, so he wasn't even sure how much his face would appear on the screen.

Perhaps he could get Karen to search for it and they could watch it later.

She'd decided they were sharing a room, but there were two beds. He'd carried her rather large bag up from the Hummer, and it was now unzipped on one them.

"I'll get changed," she said. "Then we can head downstairs."

Cthulhu blushed at the idea of her getting dressed, but turned away, and a second later the bathroom door closed. It opened a few minutes later and she stepped out into the room.

Karen wore a one piece suit, sort of. The middle was cut out of the front and back, and the ample skin of her belly showed through the gap. He was surprised to see some kind of jewelry in her navel, like a diamond or something. He sucked in a breath between his teeth at the sight.

She spun around, and he saw her back, slightly curved inward and well-tanned. Her pear shaped body pleased him, and he smiled to himself.

She turned back to face him and caught him smiling.

"You like?" she asked.

He could only manage a nod.

"Okay, let's go." She placed her overly large sunglasses on her face even though they were inside and were not likely to go out any time soon.

He walked toward the door, and she slipped her hand around his arm again. It had almost become a habit for her. She stood on her tip toes when he paused to open it and kissed him on the cheek. He blushed again, feeling his face warm.

"You're quite the hunk," she said.

He managed to get the door open, just, and they made it into the hallway. When they got to the elevator, and the doors closed on them she turned to face him. Slipping her arms around his neck, she moved her face to his and kissed him, right in the center of his tentacles. He let them slide apart, and she buried her face in them, reaching his lips with hers.

Cthulhu wanted to enjoy this, but he had a problem.

They were in an elevator, and he hated closed in spaces. His breathing accelerated and he whined just a little.

Karen clearly mistook his reaction. She pressed closer into him, and he felt her body against his. He whimpered, both from the enclosed space and the way he was becoming aroused. The feeling was odd, to say the least.

Then he felt the elevator slow and realized the ride had only lasted mere seconds. She released him and stood by his side, holding his hand as the doors opened.

He felt like sprinting for safety, but instead simply exited quickly and then took a moment to gather his breath. He put his hands on his knees and bent over, taking air in and out of his lungs.

His heart rate slowed, and he stood.

"Wow," Karen said. "I am glad to see I have that effect on you."

He smiled, not wanting to tell her the real reason for his anxiety.

"I bet you are a good swimmer," she said.

"I am," he said. "I'll show you."

They headed for the pool area, and Karen used their room key to open a locked door.

The room smelled heavily of chemicals, and Cthulhu wrinkled his nose, which caused the tentacles on his face to wiggle. He sneezed.

Two small children sat on the edge of the pool, a boy and a girl, and the girl pointed at him and giggled.

He smiled and waved back.

An adult male, probably their father, sat in one of the chairs and he looked at Cthulhu and stared. Karen lowered her sunglasses and stared at him. He dropped his gaze quickly.

"Nice shirt," was all he said.

Cthulhu nodded. "Thank you. I think I have a good chance of taking 2024."

The man laughed. "With the clown in the White House now, you may be right."

Cthulhu had watched some earth programs before leaving home, and most of the news people seemed to like the current man, and no one called him a clown. He did not even wear makeup or have big feet.

But whatever made his chances better. He daydreamed for a moment. He and Karen disembarking from a large flying device and headed across an impossibly green lawn to the big building they called the White House. The very thought was divine.

Maybe they had a pool there, too. Inside even, like this one.

Still, that smell bothered him.

But it did not seem to bother Karen at all. She dropped her towel on a chair and walked toward the water, and he couldn't help but stare.

He dropped his towel on a chair next to hers and pulled his shirt over his head. He dropped it beside the towel.

"Holy—" the father said. He motioned to his kids. "Hey, hey, I think it's time to go."

The young girl, who had giggled and pointed before, looked terrified, and ran to her father. A moment later they were gone.

"Was it something I did?" he asked.

"No," Karen said. "It's not you, it's them. Now we have the place to ourselves."

Impossibly, the smell of chemicals got stronger the closer he got to the water, and Cthulhu hesitated, but Karen waded in and held out her arms.

"Come on," she said.

So he did. He waded in and felt some kind of acidity on his skin. Karen was fine. He should be too.

He waded deeper and even lowered himself into the water. It was cool, but it felt unnatural. Still, he wanted to please her and not be a party pooper.

He lowered his body, and then ducked under the water, taking some in.

He senses rebelled. The water burned his tongue, his lungs, his nostrils.

Cthulhu shot from the water with a roar. Everything burned, and he couldn't see clearly.

He sneezed, a wet and snot filled sneeze, and then coughed, shooting water all over the side of the pool.

"What kind of water is this?" he asked when he got his breath.

"It's chlorinated," Karen said. "To kill germs."

"It nearly killed me," he said.

"Well, you don't drink in it, you just swim in it."

"Ah." He found that weird, because he could even ingest salt water and be fine, but this was different.

"Follow me," she said. She swam across the pool, the muscles of her body moving gracefully.

She swam well.

Cthulhu followed, and found if he kept his head up and didn't taste or breath the water, he was fine. In fact, this was almost fun.

It was an odd feeling for him. But he decided to roll with it. After all, what was the worst that could happen?

SIX

Gestalt Shaker and Love

The dot on the map was stationary, and had been for a while, so they made a stop at New Army, a not-quite-used-but-this-has-been-hanging-on the-rack-long-enough-to-go-out-of-style clothing outlet.

They'd outfitted Gestalt with some cargo pants, a long sleeved t-shirt, and a baseball cap that were supposed to help him look normal again. It didn't work, but it helped. Maybe.

First, while trying on a few items, an extremely large spider with eyes on tentacle like stalks came running under the door, scaring a young lady looking at rock and roll t-shirts on a discount rack.

Kansas stepped back and crushed the spider with his boot, removing it quickly. Something purple squirted from the body, smoked for a moment, burning a hole in the carpet. It smelled like a giant dog fart but dissipated quickly.

"Eww," the girl said, and continued to look through the shirts.

When Gestalt emerged, the same young girl stared at him, screamed, and ran for the front of the store, which brought the attention of someone in charge of menswear.

"What is going o—" he stopped. "My God, what is that?"

The man, or rather boy not much older than the startled girl, took one look at Gestalt and ran for the fitting rooms, where retching sounds could be heard for the next couple of minutes.

Kansas shrugged, they walked to the front counter, where he deposited a pile of tags that used to be attached to the things Gestalt was wearing.

The cashier looked at them, looked away from Gestalt, and rung them up without ceremony. As they walked away, Kansas noticed another large spider exit the leg of Gestalt's pants and scurry under the counter.

He didn't try to step on it or wait to see what happened.

Instead, they headed for the pair of trucks. The dot on the map was still stationary.

The Black Widow opened her phone and looked at a map, comparing it to the one on the screen Kansas held. She moved her phone map around using her pointer finger, and then tapped it once.

"Aha!" she said.

"Aha?" Kansas asked.

"Achoo!" Gestalt sneezed.

"Bless you," the two humans said at the same time, and then offered each other a high five.

Gestalt grunted and looked from one to the other. He then made an odd noise, one that sounded like someone being strangled and laughing at the same time.

"Ahem," the Black Widow said. "I think I know where they are."

"Where?"

"A Marriot. I bet anything that Karen lady has a discount card there or something."

"Well, they have plenty of money. We can probably stake out the place until they come out and leave."

"Well, unless we can find out what room they are in."

"And do what, Genius? Walk up and knock?" the Black Widow asked.

"Slurp." Someone was about to say something, so they turned to look.

"Gestalt will smash the door. Take Cthulhu."

"We need to find his treasure first," Kansas said. "That's the deal. Remember the plan."

The beast snorted. There was a potential roar there, and Kansas knew they would have to keep him in check, or the plan would be blown.

"You can have him soon," he said. "Very soon."

The creature smiled or moved his face into what Kansas assumed was supposed to be a smile.

"I'll follow you," the Black Widow said.

Gestalt followed Kansas to his truck, and he only hoped all the spiders had been let loose in the New Army store.

As they climbed into the truck a woman ran from the store screaming. A spider, much like the one he had crushed in the store, but more like the size of a small poodle, was close behind her.

The young manager emerged, trying to hit it, and missing quite successfully, with a broom handle.

"Let's go," Kansas said urgently, but he saw the expression again on Gestalt's face, what looked like the ghost of a smile.

He roared out of the parking lot and saw the Black Widow close behind.

The Marriot was not far, and they pulled into the parking lot nearly together. The Hummer sat just to the right of the front door, and Kansas parked right next to it. The device in his hand beeped crazily until he found out where to turn off the volume.

"Won't we be obvious sitting here?" the Black Widow's voice crackled through the radio.

"We won't be here long," Kansas said. "I'm just going to go ask the desk clerk a few questions. See if I can get some information. Then we will move."

"Okay. Don't let them spot you."

"Do I look stupid to you?" he asked.

"I won't answer that."

He started to get out and Gestalt started to follow. "No, stop."

"No stop," Gestalt said.

"Yes. Wait here. If he sees you, they will run," Kansas told him. *Not to mention the running desk clerk and other staff,* he thought.

Gestalt folded his thin arms with his oddly placed muscles over his chest. Kansas just smiled, shut the driver's door, and walked inside.

"Can I help you?" a cheery voice called from behind a large, oak desk.

"Hey there, I sure hope so," Kansas said. He took off his hat, realizing his whip was still attached to his belt. Maybe the clerk wouldn't notice.

"I'll sure try!" The man would have been a dead ringer for Mr. Rogers, but his teeth were too large for his mouth, making his chin jut forward in an unnatural way. A vertical ditch in the center of his chin looked like an indent from a well-aimed softball bat. His hair was helmet solid, swept to the side, and his eyes sparkled with genuine delight.

"A friend of mine might be staying here," Kansas said. "A large man, greenish skin, maybe a little, you know—" Kansas made a gesture indicating his face. "—different."

The clerk opened his mouth to answer, and then from behind them came a loud shriek.

"You! You!" the voice belonged to a woman, shrill and deadly as nails on a chalkboard.

Kansas turned. It was Karen. She was dripping water onto the carpe of the lobby, a towel wrapped around her shoulders. She wore an odd swimsuit, and he could see that her prominent navel was pierced.

"Get. Him. Out." She made her statement firmly, pointing a finger with each word that came out of her mouth.

"Wha—" Kansas tried to stutter out something, anything.

"This is my ex. He threatened me. He should not even be here. I have a restraining order."

59

"You do not," Kansas said, gathering his wits for a moment.

"I do, back home. You know it is true."

A glance at the desk clerk revealed that things were not doing his way. The overly large teeth were now hidden under downturned lips, and a phone was in his hand.

"Hey, hey," he said. "I'll go. I'll go. I just had a few——"

"You get him out of here," Karen roared. "You get him out, or I want to speak to the manager!"

Kansas looked left and right, and the desk clerk cleared his throat.

"I'm the night manager, sir, and this woman is one of our guests. If you don't leave her alone and leave, I'm going to have to call the police."

"The police? Why don't you just——"

"Why is he not gone yet?" Karen yelled. "Why is this man still here?"

"Okay. Okay." Kansas turned. "But you might want to ask yourself if you know who Cthulhu is. Do you know who the man—no the thing—you are protecting really is?"

"Get out!" the sound reverberated off the walls of the lobby and seemed to cause Kansas' feet to turn around on their own and propel him toward the door.

He only looked back once, and saw Karen standing, arms folded. Cthulhu was nowhere to be found.

Maybe he ditched her already, he thought. But he had a gut feeling that wasn't true.

"So, how did it go?" the Black Widow said, pointing at his face. "You look like you saw a ghost."

"Almost. I got rebuffed by a Karen."

"Did you see Cthulhu?"

"No, but he is in there, I know it."

"Well, what do we do then?"

"Change of plan. But we still stake the place out. We're going to get him, one way or the other."

Gestalt made the laughing sound again. Kansas didn't find it funny at all.

He got into his truck and drove across the street, parking behind a fast food joint where he could just keep the Hummer in sight.

The Black Widow followed, and then joined him. "So we wait? How long?"

"Long as it takes," he said. "You got night vision?"

She held up a pair of low light goggles nearly identical to his own.

He smiled. "Great minds. Well, they have to come out of there sometime."

"If Cthulhu is still there."

"Oh, he is. My bet is that he is in love."

"In love?"

"You didn't see her. That woman is pure evil incarnate. For Cthulhu, what's not to love?"

The Black Widow laughed, and then they both raised their binoculars at the same time. The light was disappearing from the sky, and unless he missed his bet, they would try to use the cover of night to escape.

His stomach growled. They'd have to take shifts to get something to eat. Maybe he could con the Black Widow into taking Gestalt this time. He wasn't sure he could stomach seeing that again.

Speaking of which, he turned to see what the creature was doing.

He was fast asleep, head thrown back, mouth open. Good. They wouldn't need him for a while.

The Black Widow looked at him and smiled.

"What?" he asked.

"I have a good feeling about this," she said. "We're about to have a good time."

He snorted, but in the pit of his stomach, he would bet she was wrong. Things were going to get a bit hairy soon, and he fingered his whip with one hand, hoping his skills would be enough to see them through.

"DID HE SEE ME?" Cthulhu asked from behind a pillar near the pool.

"No, and I got rid of him."

"How?"

Karen smiled. "I told the manager he was my ex, and dangerous, and needed to go. He won't be back."

"If he comes back, we call the police."

"Okay."

"So for tonight, we can stay put. Maybe order in?"

She sidled up next to him and slipped her arm into his. She pressed her body against his arm.

He smiled, would have giggled, but it came out as a raspy, pebble-filled grunt.

"What are you in the mood for?"

"Sushi?" he asked. "Can we get sushi?"

"Sure," she said. "We can use Window Snail."

"Window Snail?"

"It's a food delivery service. They promise to be slow, and your food will be cold when you get it."

"That works for sushi!"

"Yes," she said. "Shall we go back to the room?"

"Yes?" he said. But he found himself very nervous and suddenly very warm. He started to sweat. He wanted to attribute it to the room they were in, but that room was cool.

In fact, his sweat dried quickly but left his skin feeling clammy and just a little gross. It also felt laced with chemicals. He wondered how he would get it off, and then he remembered.

"Weren't we going to go and get me some more clothing?" What they had gotten at Off Target was not enough to last the whole week, at least according to Karen.

"We do need to do that, yes. Perhaps we can grab an Oooober, or maybe the hotel has a shuttle."

"Okay," he agreed. He would simply have to be okay with feeling a little bit gross until they returned.

Cthulhu dried himself as thoroughly as possible with a provided towel. He then pulled his Cthulhu for President shirt over his head. He stopped when he saw Karen watching.

"What a hunk," she said quietly. But he heard her and smiled.

They returned to the room, where Karen changed, making Cthulhu even more self-conscious about his clothing. She came out wearing a white blouse, a tight and short black skirt, tights, and then she slipped on some short boots to go with it.

She looked hideous in a way he found exceptionally attractive. She put on a different pair of earrings, ones that matched a large ring she wore on her right hand, and then spun around.

"Are you ready to go?" she asked.

"Of course," he said. She craned her neck up toward him and he responded by kissing her.

She responded perfectly. She parted the tentacles on his face, put her lips on his, and with her arms around his neck kept him pressed against her.

He felt her move against him, and it felt like she was trying to get even closer, to become one with him. He'd never felt this kind of physical affection, Not from Idh-yaa and certainly not from anyone else. He responded, pressing against her as well, feeling her lips moving against his. Then she broke the embrace.

"Let's go shopping," she said. "Quickly, so we can get back here."

Cthulhu had never felt such attraction to a human. He'd always harbored hate against them in general. There were a few, mostly the treasure hunters like Kansas Smith, who he reserved special and more intense hatred for.

He could have burst from hiding, overcome him, and taken him out once and for all. That would have meant fleeing to the realm of the Great Old Ones, cutting his vacation short, and explaining to them why he had interfered with human affairs in such a violent and open way.

Tearing ships asunder out in the sea under the cover of night was one thing. Tearing a human apart in a hotel lobby was quite another.

And there was Karen. He wanted to know more about her, and determine if this attraction was valid, a form of insanity, or due to the sushi he'd eaten.

Any atrocity he committed at this point would separate them forever. Oddly, he felt sadness at this thought.

So he'd remained hidden and enthralled by Karen and her response. He hadn't heard all the words, but the anger! The angst! The authority with which she spoke!

What are you thinking, Cthulhu? he said to himself. *Where are you going with this? Even if you like her, do you think she will return to the Great Old Ones with you? Would they even let him bring a human wife into their realm?*

Although Karen might be more than she seemed. She might be more eternal than he thought. Her evil would certainly extend her life beyond a normal human level. It seemed impossible that she would not live and long and productive life.

And there was little reason she could not live it with him. But would she give up what she had on earth to go with him?

He certainly could not stay here. There was little he could do about that. Not only would the Great Old Ones not allow it, but eventually his true nature would take over, and it would show. He would become something humans would seek to kill, destroy, and steal from. No, that would be impossible.

He dismissed it. He was getting way ahead of himself.

"Where were you just now? You seemed far away."

"Just thinking," he told her. "How do we find an Ooober?"

"Well, I already ordered one using their app." Karen turned her phone around to see something called a gray Camry with a creature named Al inside was approaching their position.

"You can order a horseless carriage on your phone?"

"Yes. It is not all that new. Don't you have Ooober where you come from?"

"No. The Great Old Ones would not allow this. What do you call it?"

"Ride sharing."

He snorted. "Sharing. Ha!"

Karen looked puzzled but smiled anyway. "Well, thanks to your rare coins, we have plenty of money. So we aren't really sharing, we are paying for our ride."

"If you pay, why is it called sharing?"

"Well, because—let's just say it's complicated, okay?"

"Okay. But—"

"Let's go. Keep your head down just in case Kansas and his crew are watching."

"Will do."

They went downstairs, kissing briefly in the elevator and holding hands all the way.

They exited the lobby and moved into the sunlight. They got into a gray car, what must be a Camry, and Al turned to the pair of them. "Nice costume and nice shirt," he said to Cthulhu. "Where to?"

"New Army," Karen said. "We need to do some shopping."

Al just laughed, and they drove away. About ten minutes later, they were in a huge parking lot filled with cars. Al stopped by the door, and Karen got out. "Thank you," she said.

"You were so pleasant to him, but you didn't pay him," Cthulhu marveled, wondering if she was the woman of his dreams after all.

"I paid him through the app," she said. "And I didn't tip him. I just didn't want him to know. The backseat of that car stunk something awful."

Cthulhu sniffed himself, thinking it must be him that smelled, but he didn't think his odor was that bad.

"Oh, it's not you, honey," Karen said. "You smell fine."

She emphasized the word fine, and he grinned to himself.

There she was. And she seemed to adore him.

"Let's go inside," she said. "I'm sure they have a great selection for you here."

As they entered the store, the cashier looked up at Cthulhu. Her eyes widened, but then her gaze traveled to his shirt, and she smiled. Then she laughed.

"Nice one!"

He looked down at his shirt, and then understood. He laughed, too, a sound like nails running down a chalkboard. Her face crashed, smile disappeared, but thankfully Karen broke the tension.

"Menswear?" she asked.

The cashier pointed, and the pair headed back that way. They found a section filled with shorts, shirts, and even a small section of shoes.

Cthulhu was overwhelmed, but Karen helped him, and piled his arms full of clothes in his size. He went into a fitting room and tried them on. Some worked better than others, and he modeled each combination for her.

After about 20 minutes, he had a pile of discounted clothing, including t-shirts with lettering on them, a hat, another pair of shoes, and even another pair of swim trunks.

No way would he need all of these in the short week he would be here, but selecting them seemed to please Karen, so he rolled with it.

As they were headed to the checkout stand, they saw a thin young man with glasses standing nearby. He was watching them carefully and speaking into a phone.

Karen shot him a stare, and the man turned away. Cthulhu had a bad feeling about him. He growled, and then stopped himself. He snapped his jaws together, imagining the human's fragile bones snapping between his teeth.

He was a threat. He didn't know how, but he felt it.

"Easy," Karen said. "Let me handle this, okay?"

Cthulhu backed down but remained alert. There was something here, some kind of presence, something from his world. He looked left and right, not seeing anything.

They stopped and Karen handed the pile of things to the cashier. She started to ring them up and with every beep, Cthulhu felt his heart skip.

But nothing appeared.

Karen handled the cashier the money, and she handed her some change.

"Thanks for coming," the cashier said.

"Still overpriced," Karen muttered.

She turned toward the door, and Cthulhu followed.

Then he saw it. A large, black spider blocked their way, two red eyes on stalks finding them. Karen inhaled sharply and stepped behind him.

Cthulhu stepped forward.

"Get out of the way," he said. "Now."

The spider danced back and forth, and Cthulhu advanced. Then just as suddenly as it appeared, it turned and ran the other direction. Behind him, Cthulhu heard a scream.

A pale, oddly dressed man was dragging Karen away from him, down the aisle between the racks of clothing, toward the back door.

Cthulhu roared, and lunged for him.

And then tripped.

The spider was at his feet again and lunged at Cthulhu as he fell. He grabbed the spider by the middle of its body and squeezed. Karen's screams got fainter, and Cthulhu did the only thing he knew would stop this monster.

He bit its head off.

The spider fell, writhing, to the floor, blood spurting into a large puddle on the floor.

It was black, sticky, and thick.

But he took no time to look at it or savor the taste. Instead he stood and ran. He burst through the back door, and saw a large, black truck speeding away.

Laying on the ground were the two bags of clothing they had just purchased.

But Karen was gone. Cthulhu roared at the sky, grabbed the bags, and sprinited after them.

But there was no way to catch the truck. He gave up chase and stopped.

He had no idea where to go from there.

SEVEN

Escape

"Hold her. Damn!" Kansas said.

"I'm trying!" The Black Widow was trying to hold Karen in the crew cab of the truck.

An empty soda cup with a straw dangling from the cap struck the windshield.

Gestalt turned toward the back seat, spun forward again, put his hands over his face and roared. Kansas could see a black substance oozing from between his fingers.

He slurped loudly. "That woman broke my face!"

Kansas turned his attention back to the road, trying not to swerve too erratically. The last thing he needed was law enforcement attention. From the corner of his eye, he saw a spider flee from between Gestalt's fingers and scurry under the seat.

A bag of some sort swung by his head, missing narrowly. It swung again, and he ducked, causing him to squirm. In the rearview mirror, he could see Karen was now on top of the Black Widow and beating her mercilessly with her bag. He could hear the thumps, and the grunts from the smaller woman.

"Help me Kansas! Stop the truck and get. Her. Off." Each word was punctuated by a grunt.

"Are you serious?" he said, turning his head.

"Yes!"

Beside him, Gestalt put his hands down. His face had a large, fist sized hole in it.

"Stop, and I will handle her," he said, his voice calm, but loud and strangely even. It would have been less frightening if he had roared the words.

Seeing little choice, Kansas pulled into the next parking lot and stopped the truck. Gestalt was out in a flash and yanked the back door open.

Kansas thought it was over. The creature would kill Karen, the police would come, Cthulhu would escape, and who knew what would happen to him and the Black Widow.

But it wouldn't be good. He had to stop him.

He slid from the driver's seat and uncoiled his whip as he walked around the hood.

A woman flew from the back door of the truck and landed on the ground. It wasn't Karen, but the Black Widow.

She moved, so the creature had not killed her. Karen followed, and Kansas could see the creature's hands in her hair, pulling her body into the daylight.

Karen kicked out and resisted with more strength than he thought possible. It seemed unreasonable for her to be able to resist.

But she did. She spun under her short haircut, and punched out, striking Gestalt in the gut. He roared and lunged.

But Kansas was quicker. He cracked his whip, and it wrapped around Gestalt's reaching arm. The creature released Karen's hair, and she turned to flee. She stopped long enough to kick the Back Widow, who moaned with the blow.

"Let. Me. Go!" Gestalt roared with each word, grabbed the whip, and pulled.

Kansas felt his feet leave the ground and in the next moment, he found himself in Gestalt's grasp, feet dangling. He couldn't get more than a teaspoon of air at a time through his throat.

"You let her get away!" the creature yelled.

"We can't kill her! Do you understand? She was our leverage!"

"Gah!" the creature released him and spun away.

Kansas looked beyond him. Karen was gone.

He ran to the Black Widow. Her eyes fluttered, her breath came in shallow gasps, and the side of her face and one hand were bleeding.

"We have to get rid of him," she said softly.

"I know," he said.

"We can find Cthulhu on our own."

"I know," he said. "Take it easy. I'll handle it."

"Okay." She rolled to her knees and attempted to stand up. She coughed.

Kansas reached out to help her. Once she was steady, he turned to find Gestalt. The creature was gone too. There was no sign of him, or of Karen.

"What now?"

"We start over. Let's go back to the hotel."

"Okay," she said. The pair walked back to Kansas' truck, and got inside.

HOLDING the two bags of clothing, Cthulhu ran. He didn't know how to use Ooober or summon the mysterious carriage. And they had not come far, not really. Not compared to the distances in the land of the Great Old Ones.

He could smell the hotel, even at this distance. As an explorer of the world, his sense of direction was impeccable.

His feet flew over the ground, barely touching between steps. A human was running ahead of him, strange things in her ears, and he overtook her and passed her easily. He heard her squeak a scream as he rushed by, and he glanced back to see her standing on the grassy area next to the sidewalk, staring at him.

He turned his attention forward. Varying types of horseless carriages, cars and trucks of all shapes and sizes roared by on the road next to him. Occasionally he glimpsed faces in their windows, wide-mouthed and staring as he nearly kept pace, and even passed some as they sat at traffic signals, awaiting direction from the odd and invisible gods of this world.

These he ignored, but despite his ignorance, the gods of the world must be looking favorably upon him. Perhaps they favored Karen and were willing to enable his saving of her.

Whatever the case, he arrived at the hotel not long after, and ran directly to the Hummer. He yanked the door open and slid inside. The engine caught, and then he stopped.

What now? How could he find Karen?

He closed his eyes, and asked himself one question:

What would I do? Where would I go?

Kansas had to predict his need for transportation. So he would surely have gone the other direction, and Karen? Karen would resist. She would try to escape.

So he left the parking lot and turned toward the clothing store they had come from. He reached into the bag and pulled out one of the caps and pulled it low over his eyes as he drove. He saw a large, black truck traveling the opposite direction, one he recognized. Not Kansas, but the woman with him.

What now?

If they were headed toward the hotel, Karen must have escaped. Which means she was likely trying to find him.

And they couldn't have gotten far. He squealed into the parking lot of the clothing store. In his review mirror, he saw the truck pull a U-turn. Tires squealed, but a moment later the driver was following him, but were far enough behind that he felt comfortable.

Cthulhu sped around the store to the back and took a sharp right onto the residential street he'd seen Kansas take before.

And there she was. Karen.

The blonde half of her head glistened in the sun, and light bounced off her earrings into her eyes. Her large sunglasses were crooked on her nose, her tights torn, and one of her boots was in her hand. She limped toward him.

As she saw the Hummer, her face broke into a radiant frown.

He pulled to a stop right next to her, but she ran around the front of the truck, and opened the driver's door.

"Scoot over," she said. "I'm driving."

"They're right behind us," he said as he slid over the large center console to the passenger seat.

"Not for long," she said.

Cthulhu was thrown back into the seat, and he quickly pulled the seatbelt over his chest.

Karen drove like a woman possessed, and with the Hummer, obstacles were, well, no obstacle.

Kansas was right with them at first, at least Cthulhu assumed she was driving. He stayed with them turn for turn.

Karen drifted around a corner, and the large tires chirped as they skipped over the pavement. She ran over a curb, took a sharp right, and then entered a main thoroughfare. She accelerated into the left lane, and Kansas appeared to be falling back.

Karen then did the unbelievable. There was a gravel turnout separating the westbound from the eastbound lanes, and without slowing she turned, pulled the emergency brake, and drifted into it.

Well, a clean drift would be an exaggeration. The rear tires chirped, bumped, and for a moment, he thought the wide Hummer would roll.

Just as they tipped on two wheels, she released the brake, hit the accelerator, and twisted the wheel in the direction of their fall. The airborne driver's side tires crashed to the ground with a thump, they skidded, and then she turned into the eastbound lane, accelerating up to speed with a cloud of black diesel smoke obscuring their escape.

He looked back, and saw Kansas stopped several hundred feet beyond the turn around. His reverse lights came on, but he would be much too late.

Karen pulled into the right lane.

"Are you okay?" he asked.

Karen set her jaw, and then he saw a smile form at the corner of her lips.

"Hell, yeah! That was fun!"

"Where to now?"

"Well, I was hoping you would have an idea." Her gaze told him he better, but he had been thinking.

"We get our stuff from the hotel. Then we head to Gettysburg."

"What's there?"

"A treasure, and perhaps a friend," Cthulhu said. *A friend I can buy*, he thought but didn't say out loud.

He was not the only creature from the land of the Great Old Ones who loved earth, and there was a place, a secret place that had been there since the before the Civil War. It was now obscured, part of a military reserve and a museum, but that should pose little problem.

Some creatures could take on the form of humans, and even keep that form for a long time.

"That's like three hours away," she said.

"It's a pretty drive," he said. "Except for the part through Baltimore. It will be dark though, so we won't see much. I'll drive."

"Sounds like a road trip," she said, putting her hand on this thigh. "This should be fun."

"Yes," he said. "But one more thing."

"What's that?" she asked.

"I'm hungry. Let's get that sushi for the road."

"Deal."

Karen accelerated toward the hotel in order to pick up their bags.

Cthulhu stared at her as she drove. What an amazing woman. She'd escaped, and despite the ordeal was calm, ecstatic even.

She might be the stuff of other's nightmares, but she looked like a dream to him.

EIGHT

On the Road Again

"Just a sec," Karen said after Cthulhu tossed her large bag and newly acquired small one into the back. "How did they find us?"

"Well, followed me, I guess." He licked his fingers, still able to taste the take out sushi he'd quickly consumed. Karen had only had a few pieces, declaring that she was not that hungry yet.

"How did they know where you would be?"

"Well—" Cthulhu stopped. They had found him rather rapidly after Karen had escaped. Even before that. How would they know to find them at the Marriot?

"I don't know," he finally said.

"Well, this is a former government vehicle, right?"

"Y-y-yes." Cthulhu did not actually know, but he assumed she knew what she was talking about, so seconded the comment.

"They put trackers on those. I read about this once."

Karen pulled her overly large phone from her purse, and opened a search app.

She was soon on a video site. She opened the hood after walking around the hummer. She looked around the battery, looking back at her phone from time to time. She then pulled a little box off the inside of the fender and held it up triumphantly.

"Found it."

"Good job?" Cthulhu said. "Now what?"

Karen looked around and saw a landscaping cart. It was metal and filled with various tools. She could see the landscaper's truck parked nearby.

The landscaper would wander the premises for a while maybe, but then would load this in his truck and take off. That would lead their pursuers in the wrong direction, at least for a while.

"That should do it," she said. She came over and gave him a peck on the cheek. "Let's go."

He blushed, and then slid behind the wheel.

He drove out of the parking lot, and then followed signs to Maryland 404 West. The tires buzzed pleasantly on the pavement, and after a few moments, he looked over to see Karen was asleep, her head resting on the doorframe.

The bright headlights drove a path into the dark. There was little traffic at first, and it only intensified slightly near Baltimore. He had no idea what rush hour was, other than a funny movie with a Great Old One who took the form of Jackie Chan and passed himself off as an earthly martial arts expert.

Cthulhu had seen the movies. It spoke to the gullibility of humans that they thought another human could perform those feats. I mean, who didn't know Jackie Chan and Michael Jordan were clearly not human? Sheesh.

Either way, he was missing rush hour, something related to the cars on the road, or so he surmised from the commentator on the radio. The chatter between music couldn't be any more boring.

But it gave him time to think. Think about where they were going, and why. There was another one posing as a human, not Chan or Jordan certainly, but an extraordinary person, nonetheless. Cthulhu only hoped he was still in the same place, doing the same things, and performing his other duty.

Protecting a treasure belonging to the Great Old Ones.

If he wasn't? Well, Cthulhu would have to find another way inside, or go on to the next treasure location. Just—well, his week was already passing quickly.

He came here to relax, and then he'd found Karen.

But even for his kind, a chase was not the greatest of first date choices.

The thing is, she seemed comfortable with the chaos. They were running from people who'd tried to kidnap her, he'd told her they were headed toward Gettysburg and treasure, and she just accepted it.

In fact, at the Marriot, she'd chased off Kansas and made him look like the monster, the bad guy.

He glanced down at his shirt, Cthulhu for President. He thought maybe, with her beside him, he could actually make this work. He would go home, tell the Great Old Ones he was leaving for good, and come back to earth to rule this miserable country.

Truth is he couldn't do much worse than the current group in power. He'd save money right away, as there was no need for secret service agents to surround him. He was his own security. And getting congress to follow his agenda? Please. He's simply eliminate those who were not loyal. Soon, the others would get the picture and fall in line.

The people would follow him too. He could make this country, almost the greatest evil on the planet, an even greater influence for the destruction of humanity. There was little doubt they deserved it.

Again, he looked over at Karen, sleeping peacefully behind her huge sunglasses. Her skirt had crept up and he admired her stout, well-muscled legs.

Oh yeah. She could do some damage. He would bet her kidnappers were still sore.

The miles passed under them quickly, and he soon saw a sign: "Gettysburg, 13."

That meant it was time to find a place to stay for the night. No matter how great his friend was, he didn't want to wake him this late. Besides, the place the treasure was buried was supposedly haunted. Cthulhu hated humans in general, but he hated dead people more than the general population. They were demanding, cold, entitled, and refused to leave this world and move on to where they belonged.

Annoying. They didn't even belong—

They didn't even belong here, and neither did he. Not really. Despite how popular evil had become.

Unlike those ghosts, ethereal beings clinging to the dirty surface of this worn out world, not realizing the greater evil and discomfort that awaited most of them in the beyond, he could do something about it.

He could bend this earth to his will, so he belonged, so evil ruled, and so good was the abnormal, the thing that did not belong.

It would be a lot of work.

He looked over at Karen. For her, he would do it. Stay here. Subjugate the humans. Rule in his rightful place.

Nothing would stand in his way, certainly not some silly treasure hunter and his pals. Not even Gestalt.

He gently tapped Karen on the thigh, and she stirred then woke up fully.

"Time to find a hotel," he said when she looked at him. "We're almost here."

"I'm sure there is at least some kind of Marriot around here somewhere," she mumbled, looking at the large screen of her phone. "And I hope we can get something to eat. After that nap, I'm starving."

He burped. The sushi was still sitting in his belly, but he felt like it could use some company.

Once they were headed toward the hotel, they stopped at a drive thru and got Karen a chicken sandwich and Cthulhu some fish and chips again.

He actually found himself looking forward to sleeping in a bed, with this woman.

It was an odd feeling.

"WAIT!" the Black Widow put her hand on Kansas' arm. "What are you doing?"

He stopped backing up and looked at her. "Going after them!"

"Why? Do you think they knew we tracked them because the Hummer was LoJacked?"

He snapped his fingers. "No! We can just wait and follow them later!"

He dug the tracking device from his pocket and looked at it. The map expanded as the red dot sped away, but it must be a good one, satellite or cellular connected, and he smiled.

"They're headed back to the hotel. I doubt they will stay there, but it's a starting point."

"Good call."

"Okay. First order of business. Let's get something to eat, near where they are, and then let's see if we can find our creepy friend."

"You don't want to bring him along, do you?"

"Jesus, no. I want to send him back where he belongs, quite honestly," Kansas told her. "But I would rather know where he is than have him out there running around on his own."

"Okay. If we find him, then what?"

"Well, we'll ask him nicely to go away. If he doesn't, we will ask not so nicely."

"You think you can make him do anything?"

"Nope. But I know who can."

She let the comment drop, but he could tell she was curious and didn't want to.

It didn't matter. His plan would either work, or it would not.

They drove, largely in silence, downtown. "What do you want to eat?" he asked.

"Anything but fish. And can we switch to my truck if we are not bringing spider boy along? Yours has—a unique odor."

"Sure. Maybe Cthulhu won't spot us as easily."

"Not a bad thought."

Kansas could hear his own doubt mirrored in her voice. Neither thought that switching vehicles would fool the creature they pursued, and as much as he pretended he had a plan, Kansas had no idea where Cthulhu would go next or exactly how to catch him.

Previously, he'd just been concerned with treasure. Let Cthulhu lead them to his stash, wait for him to leave, and then take it. But at this point he was fairly certain it would not be that easy.

They stopped at a pizza joint, and Kansas idly checked the app. The red dot was stationary, near the Marriot, at least he thought so.

At least they were not getting any further away.

"So, how has life been treating you, Kansas?" the Black Widow asked.

"Things have been okay. Treasure hunting has been a little slow, and I was about to take a gig at a carnival. Tricks with the whip, you know? But then I got the call of Cthulhu and delayed my starting date."

"Until when?"

"Hopefully forever."

Her thin lips parted to reveal near perfect teeth. "What's your real name?"

"Kansas."

"My god. I thought that was just because of where you're from."

"No. My dad loved his home state."

"Wow. Okay."

"What's yours? Surely your parents didn't name you after a poisonous spider?"

"No. But I rarely tell anyone."

"Why?"

"My real name is almost as bad."

"As bad as Kansas Smith? Come on."

"Worse."

"Hit me with it."

"Dusti. Dusti Rhodes."

"No freaking way!" he laughed, a huge belly laugh, and the first one he'd had in a long time.

"Told you."

"Why Black Widow?"

"Two reasons," she said quietly. She tossed her raven colored hair back over her shoulder, and he noticed how deeply green her eyes were. He'd thought they were hazel before but couldn't be sure.

"First, I'm actually a widow."

"I'm sorry."

"It's okay. My fiancé and I were excited. We wanted to be married before he shipped to Afghanistan. So we rushed it, a courthouse affair. He didn't make it back."

"That's horrible."

"I was young. I got over it, but the term widow appealed to me, so it stuck."

"Why the Black Widow?"

She threw her foot up on the table and pulled up her pantleg. She then pointed to a scar, then traced her finger slowly over it.

"The day I got the news, I was in a cave on a small island off the coast of Mexico. Dark, damp, but near the surface, so hot, you know the kind."

"I do."

"There were three of us. A local guide, another treasure junkie, and me. We found a chest, about a quarter full of gold coins. It turned out the chiefs of a local island tribe found it, told their people the caves were haunted, and had been using the money they got from the gold to keep their people in line. But there was a ritual that went with it all.

"They would only take so many coins, once a year. And they would demand a sacrifice from the tribe to receive them from the gods."

"A sacrifice?"

"There were human skeletons everywhere. Anyway, I reached in for one of the coins, and slipped on the cave floor. My foot kicked one of the skeletons, which happened to be the home of a Black Widow. It bit me. The guide applied a salve, likely saving my life, but the scar stayed."

"How did you get a local to take you into 'haunted' caves?"

"He was the younger son of the current chief. His brother was in line to get the treasure, and he would have gotten everything, leaving the younger son with nothing."

"So he figured a third, now, rather than a few coins a year would be better."

"Right. We barely escaped with our lives when the chief found out what we were doing."

"Sounds exciting," he said.

"It was." She popped the last of a pile of fries into her mouth and wiped her lips. "Ready?"

Kansas slurped the last of his Dr. Pepper through his straw and nodded. "Yep, ready."

He picked up the tracker. The dot was moving, very slowly, like it was circling the hotel.

"That makes no sense," he muttered.

"What?" she took the device from his hands. "Oh, shit, we gotta go now."

"Why?"

"I think they figured out the tracker."

"How?"

"Doesn't matter. And I may not be right. But we have to find out, or we'll lose them."

Kansas stood, and they rushed to the truck. It looked like they might be stuck with his stinky ride after all.

They bounced over the curb and out onto the street. He put the accelerator to the floor, and then backed off right away.

"What—" the Black Widow said.

Then blue and red lights filled the cab.

"We're being pulled over," Kansas said.

Now they were going to lose the pair for sure. As he watched, the red dot left the area of the hotel parking lot and accelerated away.

NINE

Nothing to Complain About

The room was adequate.

Karen called it adequate. He felt like that was saying something. They'd found a place to park the Hummer where it could not easily be seen from the road, even though they were pretty sure they were no longer being followed.

"Better safe than sorry," Karen had said, and Cthulhu again felt odd. She did that to him a lot. Feeling safe was not something he normally even cared about, but she made him care. He, too, declared the room adequate, and found that indeed it was.

The pillows were fine, if not perfect. The bed was a little too firm, and that suited him fine. They were on the second floor, and there was no third. The parking lot was only sparsely populated, and Karen had insisted that they have a room with no neighbors.

Once her bag was installed on the luggage stand, she unpacked, and then made a declaration:

"I'm going to take a shower. Then you should, too."

"Sure," Cthulhu nodded. She stretched up and kissed him on the cheek again, and then spun him toward her. She pressed up against him, pressed her lips to his tentacles, and then spun away seductively. The bathroom door clicked shut behind her a second later.

His whole body was on fire. Everything inside him wanted to join her, help her clean every part of her body. He could imagine her in there and felt almost embarrassed by even his thoughts. Then he heard a click.

She'd locked the door. Good thing. It would keep him from doing anything rash.

He pulled his shirt off and flopped his body onto the bed, staying on top of the covers. It was much too hot to burrow under them, at least to him. He grabbed the remote control and pressed a button. The television came to life, and he saw his face on the screen.

"This individual," the newscaster said, "Along with a woman named Karen is believed to be in Delaware, although the pair have not been sighted recently. Police won't say why they want to talk to them, only that they are persons of interest in an ongoing investigation."

"What's happening there behind you, Wendell?" The voice came from a petite blond newscaster, now shown in the studio.

"Well, there seems to be a protest of some kind, but it looks like—well, see for yourself."

The camera panned beyond the man, and Cthulhu's breath caught in his throat. There was a group of people, a large one by the look of things, and they were holding signs and wearing shirts, all with his image on them.

"Leave Him Alone," one sign said.

"This is My President," said another.

"Choose the Ultimate Evil," said another.

All had a logo underneath, all in red, white, and blue. "Cthulhu for President 2024" it said.

The reporter gestured to someone, and a human left the crowd. He wore thick glasses, a red and white striped shirt, and an odd stocking cap.

"Can you tell me what's going on?" the reporter asked.

The young man, who looked rather nervous and constantly glanced left and right, stammered at first.

"It's okay. What's your name?" The reporter tried to put him at ease, but it seemed an impossible task. This question made the man even more nervous.

"W-w-w-waldo."

"Okay, well, why are you here Waldo?"

"We heard Cthulhu is here, visiting earth. We're here to support him."

"Support him?"

"Yes. We want him to lead us into a new era."

"Well, I'm glad we found you, Waldo. Back to you in the studio."

"Police say if you see the pair, to call them right away. They could be anywhere in the area by now, including Baltimore and even beyond. Don't approach them, as they may be armed and dangerous."

Cthulhu turned off the television and settled back. Then he heard another click.

Karen's head emerged from the bathroom, the door shielding the rest of her body.

"Cthulhu?" she said quietly.

"Y-y-yes?"

"Join me?"

He jumped up from the bed and ran to the bathroom. She took his webbed hand in hers and pulled him inside.

Half an hour later he was clean, perhaps cleaner than he'd been in the last century, and smiling from ear to ear.

Idh-yaa had never done anything like what he had just experienced. The human body was mysteriously powerful, and Karen's had taken control of his. When they emerged from the bathroom, his stomach growled.

"Oh, worked up an appetite," she said with a grin. She used her phone to arrange a Window Snail delivery, and less than 20 minutes later, they were drinking something called a shake.

It was thick, cold, and sugary. Disgusting in the most delightful ways.

Delightful? What was happening to him?

You're in love, Cthulhu, his inner voice told him. *And it is messing with your evil heart.*

He didn't try to convince himself that it wasn't true. Arguing with oneself was not evil, merely stupid. But Karen made him feel good—good in a way he liked a lot.

"You're a wonderful—whatever you are," Karen said. "Evil in all the right places, and soft where you need to be."

"Thanks?" he said. It was strange indeed. He never thought of himself as soft at all.

"Really. After Ken, I never thought I would even think of a relationship with anyone. But you—you're different."

"Am I?"

"Tell me where you are from." It was a command, one Cthulhu felt he must obey.

"The Land of the Great Old Ones," he said. "I have lived there for hun—for a very long time. As long as I can remember."

"What about your parents?"

"Gone." He wanted to keep things simple, if he could.

"That's too bad."

They sat on the bed, side by side. She was wearing a shirt that was much too long. He imagined there was nothing, or at least not much underneath. He wore a pair of athletic shorts they had picked up at the New Army store, and no shirt.

Her bare thigh touched his, and there was a unique heat there.

"What about yours?" he asked. He found that he genuinely wanted to know.

"Mom is gone. Dad, the asshole, is still around. He and I don't get along."

"What does he do?"

"He's some kind of manager. I don't know."

"Ah," he said. "Where are you from?"

"Here and there. We traveled around a lot when I was a kid. Military brat, you know."

He didn't but nodded. It must make sense to her.

"Anyway, I settled in DC. Baltimore, really. But I recently decided to move, and I'm not sure where I'm going next."

"You could—" But he stopped. It was too soon. Much too soon.

"I could what?"

"Never mind," he said. "Let me think about that more before I say anything.

"Have it your way," she shrugged. "Any brothers and sisters?"

"Yes. A sister, Cthalhay. I think she would like you."

"I'd love to meet her."

"Really?"

"Really. I would love to meet your family and learn more about you."

He smiled and scooted backwards on the bed. He pulled the pillows up behind him and rested his head on them.

Karen followed, grabbing the remote and laying her head on his chest. She turned on the television. The same man stood there, a caption under his photo. "Dover, Delaware," it read.

"—Cthulhu was here, in Delaware. We have this footage to prove it," a man on the screen said. The cameraman apparently tried to zoom in on the screen of the phone the man was holding. There it was. Cthulhu, with Karen, exiting the Off-Target, caught on video.

"That's it folks. Evil incarnate is among us once again, in the form of a man. Again, if you see this pair, don't approach them. Contact authorities immediately."

"What is this?" Karen asked.

"Oh, yeah. I got distracted before. But, um—I'm on the news."

The camera panned out, and the crowd that had been gathered before was much larger. Everyone carried signs, some clearly hand made, and others wore shirts and hats.

"You're a celebrity!" she said.

"Of sorts."

"Well, what now?"

"We go to sleep, I suppose. Then we wake up and deal with this and the treasure tomorrow."

"Sleep?" Karen clicked off the television. "I had something else in mind."

Cthulhu slid further up the bed. A moment later the lights went out.

An hour later, they were fast asleep in each other's arms.

THE BLUE AND red lights lit the inside of the truck, and Kansas sat straight, right hand still on the wheel. He knew there were guns in the truck, he'd taken them across state lines probably illegally, but as long as he could keep the cop from searching the vehicle, they would be fine.

He gripped his license and insurance card in his left hand, ready to hand them over. His window was already down.

He practiced the speech in his head.

Whatever I did, officer, I'm sorry.

Yes sir. Of course I'll pay the fine.

Expired? No, that's not possible.

With that last thought, he raised the license and insurance to his face, and checked. Nope. Everything was legal and still valid.

He was just nervous, that was all. Everything would be fine.

The seconds ticked away and became minutes.

"What is taking so long?" he said from one corner of his mouth.

"I don't know," the Black Widow responded through clenched teeth, as if the officer behind them could see their lips moving, read what they were saying or somehow sense their thoughts.

Another minute passed. Two.

"I'm going to go see what is going on," Kansas said. "The officer should be at our window by now."

"I agree, but you don't want to get shot."

"Ha!" he said and reached for the door handle.

Just then there was a thud on the back window, and they both jumped. The Black Widow screamed.

Kansas spun, and there was the face of Gestalt, pressed against the window. He grinned.

"What the—"

A second later the creature was beside his window. It slurped. Great. It had found them, and it had something to say.

"I founth yoof. I—" It cleared its throat. "I saved you."

"What did you do with the cop?"

"The what?"

"The cop!" the Black Widow asked. "Tell me you didn't kill him."

A sound followed that, by the tipped back head, Kansas assumed was supposed to be laughter.

"No. He is in his carriage. Unconscious. I secured him."

"You—" Kansas opened the door and shoved the creature to one side, then ran for the police car. If the officer had started to run their plates, had called this in at all, which he should have, they were in real trouble here.

"Come in six-five," the radio crackled. "Please respond."

Kansas looked in the back seat and saw a large man, hand-cuffed, sprawled across the vinyl covered bench seat. He studied the double chin, the large nose, and tried to imagine what he would sound like.

Then he grabbed the mic, making his voice a little nasally and high pitched.

"Everything is five by five here," he said with no idea if that was the right protocol.

"You sure you didn't get hit in the nuts?" the radio said. He must have been close with his imitation of the officer's voice, but too high.

He cleared his throat, and tried again, a little deeper. "No, no," he said. "Just a have a frog in my throat."

"You still need that plate check?"

"No. False alarm. Just some kids."

"Roger that. Stay safe."

"Six-five, out." Kansas replaced the mic. "Yeah, stay safe," he told the unconscious officer.

He figured they had anywhere from ten to thirty minutes to get out of the area.

He ran back to the truck. The only thing he had bought them was time.

He hopped in the truck. "Hey, Dusti, we have to go get your truck and ditch this one."

She nodded, a little pale. "What—is he—?"

"No, thank God. He's fine. Just unconscious. But when he wakes up…"

"Got it."

They drove back to the parking lot where her truck was parked, she got in and followed Kansas to the back of a shopping center. He backed his truck in between two dumpsters. He pulled some boxes from beside one and put them in front of the vehicle. Not ideal, but it would stop a casual observer.

He and Gestalt ran to Dusti's vehicle. She cringed when Gestalt climbed into the crew cab, but there was little they could do about it now.

He pulled out the GPS tracker and looked at the red dot. It was stopped a couple of miles from them, off to the side of a main road.

It didn't seem right. First, the dot had moved slowly around the hotel, then taken off. While they had been occupied, the tracker had only moved a couple of miles. It couldn't be Cthulhu and Karen, unless they were just being stupid and didn't realize they were being tracked.

No, something had gone wrong. They'd either ditched the vehicle or something cleverer. But it was the only place they had to start.

Dusti drove and he rode in silence except to give her directions. Gestalt was alert, but also quiet, which Kansas was grateful for. He didn't really want to hear another gravel filled slurp followed by attempted communication. Not unless there was something meaningful there that would lead them to Cthulhu.

She pulled into the parking lot, and there was no sign of the Hummer anywhere. There were several cars near a restaurant, and a few trips up and down the aisles led them to a landscaping company truck.

"This has to be it," Kansas said.

"Indeed," Dusti answered. "Do you want to look for the tracker or wait until the truck moves to be sure?"

Kansas debated. They would wait, for sure, or they could assume Cthulhu and Karen had fled somewhere and wait to hear news of some sort to indicate where they might be.

Nothing seemed like exactly the right answer, so he shook his head. "Maybe we just need some rest."

It wasn't a bad idea. They would need to lay low, in case the police officer could describe them when he woke, but in a different vehicle, at least they would feel safer, and it had been a full day.

Then the now-familiar slurp sounded from behind him. He turned.

"Phone," the creature said, and held out a bony, translucent hand.

Kansas paused only for a second, and then handed his over. The creature took it, and studied the screen for a second, seeming to figure out how the device worked, and then dialed a number.

He spoke in a strange language, and Kansas could hear the same language being spoken on the other end of the conversation.

The conversation ended, and Gestalt held the phone out to him. The number was still on the screen, and before pressing the red end button, Kansas saw it was several digits longer than a typical phone number.

"Gettysburg," Gestalt said. "There's treasure there."

"That's three hours away," Dusti said.

Gestalt just stared at both of them.

"Right." Kansas looked him up and down. "You're sure?"

Gestalt shrugged. "It's the best idea we have."

Kansas did not ask who the "we" meant but nodded.

"I know we need some sleep, but are you okay to drive?"

Dusti nodded. "I got this."

"Well, off to Gettysburg then."

"Four score and seven minutes ago—"

"Don't start," he said. "I'm gonna sleep for a bit. Wake me if you want me to take over."

"Will do," she said.

TEN

A Buffet of Complaints

The sun woke him, and he groaned. His head hurt, and he needed some of the dark, hot beverage of this world to shake off the sleepiness.

Yesterday had been a long day.

He rolled over to find Karen gone, and he could hear the shower running. Cthulhu thought of joining her again, but decided that without an invitation, that might not work out as well as he would like. So he turned on the television again.

The story of his fans and his sighting had been bumped down in the news cycle already. It took him only a moment to see why.

Gestalt's photo dominated the screen.

"A Delaware police officer was assaulted last night by this creature, one Lovecraftian buffs tell us is Gestalt, a creature from the same land as Cthulhu. The reason for the attack is unknown, and the assailant is missing. The plate number the officer called in at the time of the attack is a Kansas plate."

The commentator rattled off the numbers, but Cthulhu did not need to hear them to know who Gestalt had been with.

Kansas.

The two of them were still working together, something that surprised him. No one got along with Gestalt. No one.

Somehow they were making it work, and Gestalt might, just might, guess where he was headed.

He couldn't worry about it now. He needed to meet up with his friend, get his treasure, and move on, go somewhere far from here preferably.

Just a few days was all he was asking for. Just a few days with no one chasing him, no one nagging him, just relaxing.

The news moved on. There was a short mention of his name, and his followers, which made him smile, and then the weather came on.

Today was supposed to be clear, but thunderstorms were expected here and in Harrisburg tonight.

Great, actually. That would be fantastic cover. No one would be out in the storm. No one but him, his friend, possibly Karen, and the ghosts.

Oh, yes. The ghosts. The most haunted battlefield in the United States was a great place to hide treasure, and the ghost of a felled horseman guarded both his makeshift grave and the trunk of gold.

He was something Cthulhu could deal with. Not that he wanted to.

He would need to warn Karen, as gently as possible.

A second later she emerged from the bathroom, dressed and smelling delightful.

What a word. Delightful. He'd never used it so much in his life. Ever. About anything, let alone anyone.

He moved to her, and she embraced him.

"Anything interesting on the news?"

"Not really. I do have some things to tell you. Let's say over breakfast?"

"Sure," she said. "Get dressed."

Cthulhu reluctantly removed his Cthulhu for President shirt. But he couldn't wear the same thing forever. He grabbed a change of clothes and moved into the bathroom himself.

With a washcloth and soap, he lightly cleaned himself. There was no reason to be foul-smelling evil. Plain evil was bad enough, and with Karen by his side, he wanted to be something she was proud of. He even popped open a tube of toothpaste, something he had seen Karen do, and took a small brush from the holder. It was wrapped in plastic, and he unwrapped it gingerly. Then he went to squeeze some of the white substance onto it.

But not carefully enough. He squeezed the strange tube much too hard, and the paste went everywhere, all over his hands and the counter. He tried to wipe it off with a towel, but it was quite sticky.

He licked it off his webbed fingers and found it to be way too strong and minty. He rinsed his mouth using a small cup, swishing water and spitting.

"What are you doing in there?" Karen asked from outside the door.

"Just getting ready," he answered. He took a deep breath and looked at the tiny brush. He put it into his mouth, between the tentacles surrounding it, and moved it back and forth. It did nothing except put more of the minty foam in his mouth. Which now, shoved into his cheeks rather than licked from his fingers, started to foam on its own.

"Ugggghhh!" he said, resulting in a stream of foamy saliva exiting his mouth and coating the mirror.

"I'm coming in," Karen said.

"I'm fi—"

The door burst open, and Karen stopped and stared. He realized how ridiculous he must look. Still shirtless, he held the small toothbrush between two webbed fingers. The paste was everywhere, including the mirror, and the counter, and foam dripped from between his lips. The clothes on the counter were dotted with bits of toothpaste too, and he figured he must look totally ridiculous.

But she stopped staring and started laughing. He joined her, and soon they were both doubled over. He could not remember the last time he had laughed this hard or felt such joy.

Joy. Blech. What was happening? Why did he feel this way?

Once they stopped laughing, Karen helped him get cleaned up.

"Rinse," she said, handing him a cup of water, and he did, with that cup and then two more.

She cleaned off his clothes too, gently dabbing them with a washcloth and removing the minty stuff. In some cases it left a small residue behind, but it would be fine. They were just going to breakfast and then he would connect with his friend and make a plan.

Maybe they could take in the sights. Harrisburg was a nice place. They could walk by the river, see the capitol building.

"Where do you want to eat?" he asked.

"Do you like eggs? Breakfast food?"

"Sure," he said, feeling less than sure. But the longer he was with this woman, the more he liked human things. So he would give it a try.

"There's a Lenny's nearby. Let's go there."

After he was dressed, she gave him another once over, and then they headed out the door.

"What did you want to talk to me about?" she asked.

"We can talk about it over breakfast," he said. "I'm starving."

The sunlight seemed brighter, the breeze more refreshing as they headed toward the Hummer. He tilted his head toward the sky. The only thing that would make this day better would be the thunder and lightning coming later.

He couldn't wait.

"DUSTI RHODES. SERIOUSLY."

"I wish you would just call me the Black Widow again," she said.

Kansas stood and stretched. He couldn't say that the Motel 11 they had found late in the evening had been the best choice, but it had been one of the few options right off the freeway, and close enough to Gettysburg to mean their morning commute would be short. His back was stiff, his legs cramped from all the driving and running yesterday, and he felt a couple of bruises where Karen had struck him.

He didn't have much of a plan. Gestalt had stayed in the truck, and they hadn't ventured out to see if he was still there or if he had wandered off this morning.

"Well, I could I suppose."

"Thank you," she said. She stood from the little table in his room and stretched too. She was much more flexible than he was. She reached for the sky, then bent to touch her toes. She'd insisted on her own room but joined him in his before they sought out breakfast and decided on a plan.

She was dressed in all black again, and although her clothes looked clean, he could tell no difference from what she's worn the day before. Black lace up boots, jeans, a black V-neck shirt, and a matching jacket, unzipped and resting on her shoulders.

She straightened, poppeded her neck, and then looked him in the eyes.

"Are you staring at me?"

"Um, no. Not really. Just thinking."

"Ah. Dangerous."

"Indeed. I'm just wondering what's next."

"Do you think we can trust Gestalt?" she sat back down at the table, and he did the same, although the chairs were unforgiving and awkward.

"No."

"That was a quick answer. Why did you let him come with you anyway?"

"At the time, I thought we had a shared agenda, but we don't. He wants to return Cthulhu to his world where he belongs. I want to make sure we get some treasure first."

"Okay. How do we solve that?"

"I don't know yet. He promised to let me get the location of the treasure before he took Cthulhu away. But I'm not sure he will, and I'm also not sure he's even a match for the beast."

"Agreed." She sat back, stared into space, and crossed her legs. "First, we need some breakfast. Then we need to learn what Gestalt knows. Once we learn that, we can work on getting rid of him."

"It's weak. Not really a plan, but I don't see we have any choice."

"Is this treasure Cthulhu has hidden worth this risk?"

"Think of it this way," Kansas said. "The coins he sold cleaned the coin dealer out of his cash. The ones Gestalt has are of equal value. What if we found a chest with even fifty pounds of those coins? Other jewels and treasure from shipwrecks?"

"Millions. But would it actually belong to us?"

"Well, we might have to be sly about how we sell it, so we have less obligation to disclose how we got it."

"You have thought this through."

"Yes. Thoroughly. This is what I live for. Finding treasure."

"Me, too," she said. "I've always admired you, if from a distance."

"It is amazing we have not been on the same searches before."

"It's a big world. There are a lot of treasures to be discovered."

"Some closer to home than we think," he said. He found himself mesmerized. Relationships were not his thing, but

Kansas felt drawn to this Black Widow, Dusti, whatever she wanted to be called.

There would be time for sentiment later. For now, he felt an urge to get going. Time was short.

"I'll go get my stuff from my room," she said. "I don't have much. I'll be back in like five minutes. Then we can get going."

"Sounds good," he said.

He gave her his spare key to get back in and turned on the television after the door closed behind her.

His license number was front and center under a news reporter, talking about an attack on a Delaware police officer. Three hours away, this was news?

Then he saw the sketch of Gestalt on the screen. Followed by a story about Cthulhu supporters gathering in Dover. It seemed surreal.

They were carrying signs, wearing t-shirts with the name of the monster on them. "Cthulhu for President," many said.

He heard the door lock click behind him. "Talk about a birth certificate controversy," he muttered, turning around.

Dusti stood there, with Gestalt. "He caught me in the hall," she said. A bag, black of course, dangled from her hand.

The creature stared at him, red eyes seeming to bore into his skull. "We must go. I know where to watch," it said. "We catch him today."

"Okay. But we need to be careful. Look at this." Kansas pointed to the television.

The story about Cthulhu was wrapping up, and a weatherman took over, promising a clear day, but thunderstorms tonight.

"Just a sec," he said. He pulled up the local channel's social media on his phone, and pressed play on the first story.

There was Gestalt's face.

"Damnit!" Dusti said.

"We need to disguise him," Kansas said.

Gestalt looked from one to the other, clearly uncomfortable.

"We have to hide your face. Make it so you don't look so much like, well, you," Dusti said.

"You still have his bag of clothes?" Kansas asked.

"In the truck."

"I'll go get them." He ran down to the truck, well aware of how uncomfortable she might be alone with the creature, but not overly worried. He grabbed the bag from the back seat of her truck and rushed upstairs with them.

Dusti took a cursory makeup kit from her bag and sat the creature down. She did what she could, but finally declared, "We need a costume shop or something."

"We'll look for one later. Is he good to go for breakfast?"

"Let's see."

They dressed him in a long sleeved shirt, jeans, and high top sneakers. Dusti plunked a dark baseball cap on Gestalt's head and pulled it down over his eyes.

"It will have to do."

"Find Cthulhu now," the creature said.

Kansas and Dusti shared a look. "Yes. But we have to eat first."

The creature nodded. "Hungry," it said, voice clearer than it had been before, now milder in tone and without the gravel underneath.

"Okay. Where do you want to go?"

"Lenny's," Dusti said. "You can always count on friendly service and mediocre food that won't give you the runs."

"Done. Afterward, we'll find a place to get this one a better disguise."

"Perfect."

The trio headed downstairs, got into the truck and headed for the nearest Lenny's.

Kansas was looking forward to coffee. Nearly any coffee really.

They were so close. Today was going to be a great one. He could feel it.

ELEVEN

Managing Expectations

The food was awful. There was no other way to describe it.

And not the kind of awful Cthulhu liked, either. The coffee was lukewarm. In fact, lukewarm could describe everything, including the five dollar glass of fresh squeezed orange juice.

Karen grimaced as her supposed-to-be-sunny-side-up egg dangled off her fork. The yolk was solid and clearly dry.

"So anyway," he told her. "The treasure is in a not-so-nice-place. In fact it's—"

"It's what?" she said, toying with her hash browns. She looked around the table, picked up the salt and pepper, and a small bottle of hot sauce.

Cthulhu watched her movements carefully. He tried putting a bit of his country fried steak in his mouth, and chewed slowly, not from consideration, but because it was so rubbery he couldn't manage to get it down his throat any other way.

He managed to swallow. "The place is haunted."

"Haunted?"

"Have you heard of the most haunted battlefield in America?"

"Yes."

"The treasure is there, underground. It is guarded by a soldier astride a large horse."

"A ghost horse?"

"That's right."

"And he will let you get the treasure?"

"Yes, he will. He—my friend knows how to deal with the ghosts."

"Tell me about your friend." She put a forkful of the now salted, peppered, and hot sauces potatoes, and then spit them back into her napkin.

"He is an Old One. He has been leading the ghost tours for over forty years now. Those who knew him at the start of his job here wonder that he is still alive. He looks much the same as he did that first tour."

"He does not age?"

"Not the same way humans do."

"No one suspects him?"

"There is a lot of turnover in the tourist industry. He manages to survive."

"And these ghosts are real?"

He took a moment to consider how to answer as he lifted a fork full of scrambled egg to his mouth. He spotted something long and thin dangling from the fork, and grabbed the end, pulling it out. It was a long, curly hair.

He looked around for a waitress, but theirs was nowhere to be found. In fact, he did not see any serving staff at all.

He set the hair aside and pushed the food away from him.

"Yes. They are very real. Humans have an odd penchant for clinging to life even long after it is over."

"Indeed. I know this to be true."

"Places where violence occurs, violence like a war, are even worse. I understand this battle was especially gruesome.

"Why does your friend stay here rather than returning to your land?"

"He likes it here. At first he was in love—" Cthulhu stopped himself. "He was in love. That is why he stayed."

Karen smiled at his embarrassment. "Would you ever consider staying?"

"I-um—" He stopped. He thought of the t-shirts and signs. He thought of the pain of his home, and what awaited him there. He thought then of Karen.

He hardly knew her, yet he had, in many ways, fallen for her.

And he must decide what to do about that.

"I might," he said slowly. "If I could. The Old Ones might not be as content to leave me here as they have the old man. I have—responsibilities."

"I see," she said, staring at her plate. "This is awful."

"Agreed," he said. "We need something else to eat. I can't even finish this, and I like bad food. Usually."

Just then he saw a waitress who seemed disinterested and almost bored. He signaled her to come over, and she did.

"Hey," he said. "Our food is cold."

"Oh," she said. "Do you want me to have the kitchen warm it up for you?"

"No," he said.

"We'd like to speak to the manager," he and Karen said at the same time.

"Alright," the waitress said, and walked away.

"Jinx," Karen said. "We said that at the same time."

"We did," he said, letting her take his hand. "Where should we go from here?"

"I don't know, but I am not paying for this slop." She let her voice rise, and Cthulhu saw a manager approaching.

He wore a striped shirt, a stained tie, and looked like he had been skimming off the buffet for about five years or so.

"Can I help you?" he asked.

"Yes, this food is terrible."

"Oh, well, sorry. Do you want us to heat it up for you or something?"

"No. We aren't paying for this. We're going somewhere else."

"We can make it again for you, but you have to pay."

"No we don't."

"Um, yeah. You do." The manager folded his arms. "You pay for your food, or I call the police."

"Call them," Karen said. "Because this food is a crime. In fact, I'll call them myself."

"No, you won't. What would you like instead of what you have?"

"Nothing. Not from that kitchen."

"You have to pay then."

Cthulhu had just about enough of their banter. He stepped between them, turned to the manager, and roared in his face.

"What the—" the manager stumbled and fell backward, landing seated in a booth.

Cthulhu stepped forward. "Not only will you not charge us for this meal, but you're going to give us a gift card for next time."

"Hey, you're him!" the manager said.

"Then you know what I can do to you."

"Y-y-y-y-es. How much would you like a gift card for?"

Cthulhu turned to Karen.

"Thirty dollars."

"Deal," he said. "Just don't—"

"We'll have that gift card and be on our way," Karen said with authority. She glanced at Cthulhu, and he gave her a smile. She shook her head and scowled.

The manager rushed to the register, pulled a gift card out and handed it over.

"Thanks," Karen said. "We were never here."

"Right. I didn't see a thing."

They left, and once they got to the Hummer, Karen turned on him. "What was that back there?"

"What do you mean?"

"I had him under control."

"No, you didn't. I just wanted to get it over with. I was helping."

She looked him up and down. "I didn't need your help, or the help of any man or—whatever you are."

"What do you mean by that?"

"I mean he's going to talk. He may not call the cops, but if he tells anyone he saw you, we will have crowds following us around. You saw the news."

He had, and she was right. But he didn't want to tell her that.

"We will be fine."

"Until Kansas watches the news too, and shows up right behind us."

"Okay, okay," he said. "I'm sorry. I was wrong." He conceded. That felt odd, not like him. *Could he truly be himself with Karen?*

He'd wanted to destroy the manager, decimate him for daring defy his greatness and argue with is lady friend. She was happy with a yelling match and a gift card.

If things were going to work between them, they would need to find a middle ground.

He started the Hummer and they drove out of the parking lot in awkward silence, until they got to the Gettysburg Museum and Gift Shop.

"Is this where your friend works?"

"Sort of. But it is where we book the tour," he said. He could see by her expression she was still unhappy.

"And I really am sorry," he said. "I don't want you to be mad at me, and I don't want to fight."

"You mean it?" Karen asked.

"Yes," Cthulhu answered. She leaned over, and this time he turned his head and met her lips with his.

They hugged, kissed, and then got out of the Hummer to head inside.

The air was humid and thick, and even though he couldn't see any clouds forming, he could feel the storm brewing.

———

THE TRUCK BUMPED over the curb as they pulled into the Lenny's parking lot. Kansas looked back at the disguise Gestalt was wearing and sighed. It would have to do. He wondered how Cthulhu was blending in, especially with all the excitement about his arrival. People were likely looking for him actively now, and it would be hard to keep any appearance he made out of the news.

It made him wonder if Gestalt was right. The last sighting of Cthulhu, at least verified one, had happened in Delaware. Would he really come here for treasure and risk being exposed?

The answer was yes. The only thing Cthulhu liked better than evil was money, the love of which was the root of his favorite thing. He would come here, or somewhere he had treasure. If Gestalt's information was good, this was the place they would catch him.

Gettysburg and even the surrounding areas were small compared to the big cities surrounding it. There would be nowhere easy for him to hide.

Unless he got the treasure and became extremely more mobile. Cthulhu was cunning. He would get rid of the Hummer, get something less conspicuous, and what?

That he didn't know for sure, and not knowing made him uncomfortable.

"Well?" Dusti said.

"Well, what?" He realized he'd been daydreaming, gazing into space.

"Are we going in, or are we just sitting here?"

"Going in," he said, and got out of the driver's side. Dusti followed, Gestalt not far behind.

They went inside the restaurant, and the hostess greeted them.

"Hey folks! Three of you?"

She could count. That might be a good sign.

"Yep," he said.

The waitress led them to a table, sat out three coffee cups, three worn menus, looked oddly at Gestalt, and then said, "I'll be back shortly."

She disappeared, and Kansas looked at Dusti. "Do you think she recognized him?"

"Nope. She's not that good at hiding things. I can tell. She would've freaked if she did."

"I hope you're right."

It took a few minutes before coffee arrived. It was in a carafe, and after pouring three cups, she sent it down on their table. It steamed, Kansas took a sip, and found it to be hot and good.

"Y'all decided yet, or you want me to give you a few minutes?"

"A few minutes," he said.

They looked over the menu. He decided on an omelet, Dusti chose a skillet of some sort, and Gestalt simply said, "Same," while pointing to what she ordered.

The waitress came back quickly with waters, surveyed their coffee and topped them off with the carafe on the table.

"Did you get a chance to look things over?"

"Sure did," Kansas said, and ordered for all of them to keep her focus on him and not Gestalt.

"Coming right up," she said, and disappeared.

"She's pretty attentive," Dusti said.

"More than I would expect," Kansas said.

A thin man in a striped shirt, half untucked, walked over. A tag on his shirt read, "Manager."

"Everything good for you folks here?"

"So far," Kansas said. They didn't even have food yet.

"Good, good. Do let me know if there is anything I can do to make your experience a great one."

They watched him walk off, join the waitress by the kitchen, and turn to point back at them. She gave them a nervous glance, turned back to him, and gestured with her hands.

Their behavior was odd to say the least, including the manager speaking through the little window behind the counter to a barely visible person he assumed to be the cook.

"So, Gestalt," Kansas said. "Where is this treasure?"

The creature shrugged. "Gettysburg." His speech was clearer, and free of its former slurp and death rattle.

"We know that," Dusti said. "Can you narrow it down a bit?"

The creature looked up from under his hat, and Kansas hoped the waitress or the manager did not see the red eyes or the pale face barely hidden by makeup.

"No, I can't," he said. "You get your treasure. I get Cthulhu. That is the deal. You cannot do this on your own, and you won't leave me behind."

"We wouldn't think of it," Kansas answered.

"Liar," Gestalt said. "But that is the nature of our relationship. Since I took off on you, then the policeman, yes?"

"Yes." Kansas saw no reason to lie.

"I cannot expect you to trust me, and I in turn don't trust you. But we must work together for this to work even short term. I assure you, once Cthulhu reveals the location of his treasure, you may have it. For I will grab him and transport him away before he knows what happened. If I do not, he may have a chance to fight me. And as much as I would like to believe I am his better, I might just lose. Especially if he—"

"If he what?"

"Never mind. He will not get the chance."

The very idea sounded ominous to him. He wanted to find Cthulhu's treasure. Take it from him even, but he preferred to live through the process. If they were caught, and Gestalt could not protect them, they could easily be destroyed.

Cthulhu ate treasure hunters like him for breakfast, literally. Or really anytime. Kansas didn't think he was that picky.

The only advantage they might have would be Karen. The beast might not want to reveal his true nature to her, so might keep his humanoid form. That might spare them, at least for a few moments.

Hopefully either Gestalt would succeed, or that few moments would be enough.

The waitress returned quickly. Their food was hot, steaming hot, and the hash browns looked fresh, probably the freshest he'd ever had at a Lenny's anywhere.

"This is remarkable," he said. "Everything looks great."

She sighed in relief. "I am so glad to hear that."

"Are you okay?" Dustin asked her.

"Well, yes. The manager is really on us. A customer this morning scared him to death, I think."

"Scared him?" Kansas and Dusti said together.

"Yeah. He was a big guy, with a really upset woman. They hated their food. That's not that unusual, to be honest. This isn't the greatest restaurant in town."

"Humph," Kansas said. From the corner of his eye, he could see Gestalt's plat was already half empty.

"But people don't expect much either. These two refused to pay, and when the manager offered to replace their food instead, the big guy roared at him."

"Roared?"

"Like a lion, but not. It's hard to describe. The manager scrambled to the register, gave them a gift card, and the two of them left."

"That is odd. Do you remember either of their names?"

"Yeah. The woman, I think the guy called her Karen."

"Karen?"

"And—" she leaned closer and whispered. "The guy looked like that creature on the news in Delaware the past couple of days."

"Cthulhu?" he said.

She nodded.

"Thanks for the information. And tell your manager not to worry. The food is great, and we plan to pay for all of it, plus a great tip."

She smiled. "Thanks." She scurried away, probably intent on telling her manager he could relax.

Gestalt looked at both of them from his nearly empty plate as they dug in to their own meals.

"See? I told you so."

Kansas tried to smile, but he couldn't. The makeup on Gestalt's face had run horribly, and he had some kind of vegetable stuck in his teeth.

But it was good news. Cthulhu was here. Then he had an idea.

It wouldn't take long for the word to get out. Especially if he helped it along. And that might just work to their advantage and get rid of Gestalt at the same time.

He dug in and had to admit this was one of the better omelets he'd had in a long time.

TWELVE

Friends of Friends

C thulhu walked into the museum and up to the front desk. Karen had her hand wrapped around his arm, which felt appropriate.

The museum was a large, oddly shaped building with a theater and several exhibits inside. The real attraction for most people was outside though, the battlefields of Gettysburg itself.

The time it depicted in American history was gruesome even to Cthulhu. The one thing he savored, craved from this world was freedom: the freedom to move about, do what he wanted, and not be governed by anyone. Were he to rule this world, or any world really, he would instate this right away. Chaos and anarchy came with a price, true, but everyone could do whatever they wanted with no rules.

Evil thrived on chaos, true. But it also thrived on iron handed rule. These were the two schools of thought when it came to wickedness, and Cthulhu was a fan of the former. Chaos, anarchy, and everything that came with them were much better than any rule by the Great Old Ones, or anyone else were he to be honest.

And there it was. The noble traits of the chaotic evil were honesty and embracing the truth. There were no gods, just some beings that were more powerful than others. And all of them craved power of one sort or another. Bending others to their will was simply easier.

Some were crafty, and whole religious systems were built around the myth that they were benevolent and wanted only good for those who followed them. But their motives were always revealed. They demanded loyalty and sacrifice, and any deviation from their plan would be met with eternal punishment and misery, or in some cases earthly punishment.

And they all sought to divide the world. There would still be chaos and anarchy surrounding their followers. It was essential. A united people could easily see through the myths of any religion if they chose to be kind to one another and embrace feelings of unity, focus on the similar rather than the different, and work together to solve problems.

Disgusting.

The gods all sought to divide. It's what made their ideas possible. If their followers felt that they were superior to the followers of any other god, it was a simple matter to turn those followers on the so named "different ones."

The name of the different ones, from heretics to the ridiculous moniker "the world" adopted by some sects (as if there were a separate world within theirs, and humans did not all live on the same crowded and now stuffy planet) didn't matter. If "they" would not convert to following the "true" god, they would need to be despised at the least, eliminated at the worst.

This chaos and division caused the followers of each god, or even those with no god to cling more tightly to their own beliefs, finding it impossible to see the viewpoint of others. Therein lay the beauty of both iron rule and the chaos theory.

Eventually, the people of this world went to war with each other. They killed in the name of gods, who were no more divine than they were. Since divinity lived in everyone, it astounded him how humans could not see this, and even refused to acknowledge it. They missed out on so much. But the chaos pleased the gods. It gave them even more power, and any offer to "save" their followers was met with adoration.

That's what Cthulhu loved about Karen. She didn't seem to care for adoration. She would throw chaos into anywhere, like the Lenny's this morning, as long as it furthered her own agenda. In a way she was a goddess among ordinary women, and they would only aspire to be as powerful as she was. Any hatred of her was born of jealousy.

Cthulhu was rare among the Great Old Ones. He didn't want adoration, power, or any such baubles or sacrifices. He simply thrived on the chaos and fear itself. A fearful human, consumed, had a unique flavor. Seeing them flee made his stone heart harden further. He was hated by some too, usually out of jealousy and misunderstanding.

Some on this planet acknowledged their understanding with signs and shirts. They knew chaos would serve their freedom, and they craved it. Evil, not evil? That was all relative when it came to satisfying their own wants and needs.

Evil didn't kill love. Division did. Evil simply laughed and sought to feed the things that drove division. And true good? Please!

It was no match for evil. There was too little of it in the world to be an actual threat.

What he felt for Karen was true good, but only because of her true evil. So he felt no guilt about it. As long as they both retained their freedom, what did it matter to anyone how good or evil they were together?

His musings were broken as Karen paid their admission, and they started toward the first set of exhibits.

This war, the things this museum spoke of, were about division. It was supposed to have ended with the war, but it did not.

The more he saw, the more ne realized how much evil thrived in this country not because of the outcome of the war, but because it had never ended where it mattered, in people's hearts.

That fact made him glad. There was hope for the destruction of this unity-claiming nation, and all he or anyone like him had to do to make it happen was push it along, give it a hand, so to speak.

He did like the cannons and the way they'd been used. The crude weapons of this time were ideal for chaos and pain. This war had birthed some of the most gruesome injuries humans had ever inflicted on one another and had kickstarted the war machine that would drive the growth of America during the next century. That had been a good time for Cthulhu and his people.

Karen found things fascinating, but not in the same way he did. He could tell when she was bored and wanted to move on, and he accommodated her.

They went outside, and she took a selfie of them facing a battlefield and with one of the cannons. They then picked up a self-guided driving map of the battle grounds and set out in the Hummer again.

They got looks from time to time, and they chatted about various things they saw, imagined the ancient battles, and smiled. Then they rounded a bend.

"Here," Cthulhu said, pointing at the map. "This is where we will come tonight."

"Do you see your friend?"

"No. He will start his work in the evening, but we will go to his house after this. I just wanted to see if things had changed at all here and get a feel for the area in the daylight."

"Why can't we just take the treasure now?"

"It is guarded by the horseman. If we took it during the day without asking, all the treasure would be cursed."

"What kind of curse? Death?" Karen asked with a smirk.

"No. Much worse. Death would be simple, and instant. Suffering, misery, and eternal life."

"Eternal life?"

"As great as that sounds to you humans, it is indeed a curse."

"Are you immortal?" she asked.

He stopped. He really didn't have an answer to that, except 'sort of.'

"Can I be killed?" he said aloud. "Yes, but it would take a great deal of power. Can I be injured? Yes. But if I do not encounter such power that will kill me, I won't age or die of natural causes, if that is what you mean."

"So you don't even feel sick?"

He shook his head. "No, I feel sick much of the time, and I experience pain. It just does not matter to me the way it does to many. Pain and sickness are constant companions. I cannot imagine my life without them."

As he talked, they grew closer to a rock formation of sorts, consisting of several large rocks with deep cracks between them. They seemed almost unnaturally close together, and toward the right side, there was a large stone sitting atop the others. He grinned.

"There it is. The horseman has kept his promise."

"That's good, right?"

"Shortly, tonight, we will have in our hands the key to doing whatever we want. For the next week, maybe longer, you my dear will live like a queen. My queen."

"A week? What happens then?"

"Well, I will likely have to return to my world at that time."

"A week. As your queen?"

She emphasized the word "your."

He opened his mouth to speak. "What I mean is—"

"I belong to no one," she said. Her look of hatred bored into him. "And if a week is all you have to offer, then we have an issue."

"But I—"

"You thought I understood that this was just a fling? Is that right?"

"Well, no. You see, I—"

"Can I go with you when you leave, should I want to?"

"Maybe. I will have to—"

"And as my own person? Not a possession or a trophy?"

"Well, that part yes. I would never want you to think—" The road ahead meandered around the rocks, and he followed it.

"You better figure it out mister." Karen turned to face forward and screamed, "Look out!"

Cthulhu slammed his giant foot on the brake. The Hummer slid to a stop, inches from a man in the roadway, waving.

Cthulhu waved back.

"Who is that?" Karen asked.

"Davey. Davey Jones. Come meet my friend," Cthulhu said.

"Our conversation is not over," she said. "Not by a long shot."

"I understand. And I promise to think about what you have said," he told her.

And he would.

But for now, it was time to talk to the only man who could help them make his plans a reality.

He opened the door and stood. "Hey, Davey," he said. "Long time no see. Anyone written any new songs about you lately?"

"Nope. And I'm not running for president either. Can I get a ride back to my place? I think it would be best if we talked there."

"Sure," Cthulhu said, and Davey looked through the window. "Who's that?"

"Karen. She's with me."

"For now," Karen said as the new arrival came around the truck. "Nice to meet you."

Davey shot Cthulhu a look and climbed in the back seat.

"You still in the same spot?"

"Yep. Kids won't let me move," he said.

"Kids?" Karen asked.

"You'll see, soon," Davey said. "On Jeeves. Take me home."

Cthulhu smiled and drove forward, but a part of his mind was still on the conversation he and Karen had been having.

He felt like next time she raised questions, he better have answers, or he would find himself in danger indeed.

<hr/>

OUTSIDE, the hair was hot and thick. Thunderstorms were coming. The only question was how bad they would be, and how wet they would get.

But Kansas now had a plan. Once he knew where the treasure was, he would simply give the local news a tip, and drop a few simple posts on social media, hashtag #Cthulhu2024, and sit back and watch the fun. With both otherworlders out of the way, he would have one of the greatest treasures of all time, and he would win some serious cred in the treasure hunting community.

Hunts would just come to him after that. Everyone would want him on their expeditions. It would be a dream come true.

And he looked at The Black Widow, the infamous Dusti Rhodes. He liked her, and she might even like him, although it was hard to tell in this environment. Relationships formed under pressure were often suspect, but then both of them lived lives of pressure, so it was hard to say if this circumstance was what either of them called unusual.

"Where to, Gestalt?"

"We need to do some scouting," he said.

"First, you need a better disguise," Dusti said. "Let's take care of that first."

"Good idea," Kansas replied. Not because he didn't want Gestalt to be caught, he just did not want him to be caught until he was ready.

That meant being careful until then. He did a quick search on this phone, and found Costumes by Sally was nearby, or at least within about 20 minutes driving distance.

They had time. Gestalt seemed to think Cthulhu would move at nightfall, and although breakfast had been later than normal, it was still before noon. It would be hours before they needed to be ready.

Gestalt also wanted to scout things out, but that should not take long. He wondered why, if Gestalt knew where it was, they could not just go take it now, and leave the creature to catch Cthulhu on his own. But he figured there must be a reason.

"There is a costume store nearby," he said. "Let's go. I'll leave you in charge of that Dusti."

"Sounds good."

He started the truck and drove away. The directions led him to a freeway for a few miles, and he took a nondescript exit. The shop was in a small strip mall, and he parked a little way from the door.

"How should we do this?" he asked Dusti. "If we bring him in with us, and someone recognizes him—"

"If we don't, and the costume we choose doesn't fit, once it touches his skin, it will be pretty useless. We can't return it."

"I go in," Gestalt settled for them. "I will be careful."

His speech was clearer, but it still awkward at times, with missing articles and other words, like anyone who spoke a second language.

He didn't like it. Without Gestalt, they might find Cthulhu. It was a small area. But they might not, and if that window closed he could end up going home empty handed.

That would leave him swinging whips at a carnival and doing tricks at rodeos. That idea did not appeal to him at all. He shot Dusti a look.

He could read that she had similar thoughts, but he had no idea what else they could do. So she shrugged.

"Alright. But you stick with us. No funny business. This type of store is usually busy only one or two times a year, so we get in, get out, and get on our way. Agreed."

The creature nodded.

The trio headed through the surprisingly full parking lot toward the door. A bell dinged overhead as they walked inside. There were people everywhere, most dressed in old military uniforms and carrying swords. A salesgirl excused herself from a small group and approached them.

"Hi there," she said. "Sorry about that. We're a little busy, with the reenactment coming up tonight."

"Reenactment."

"They happen often, but this is the 160th anniversary of the battle at the Devil's Den. You didn't know?"

"Of course we knew," Dusti said. "We're just kidding you."

"Oh, ha ha." The girl did not seem to be amused. "What can I do for you? Can I direct you to something specific?"

She looked Kansas up and down and smiled, then turned to Gestalt. "Well, well, well. You already have a great start on one of the Civil War ghosts. That is unusual. Want me to find you a uniform?"

Dusti cleared her throat. "What about me?"

"Do you want to—" The girl blushed. "I mean, you don't look like the rich battle spectator type, so are you looking for a soldier uniform? For you and your—boyfriend perhaps?" She indicated Kansas.

"Oh, we're not—" Dusti stopped. "Yes, my boyfriend. This is our friends son, Jerry. He really does want to be a ghost."

Gestalt shot Dusti a slightly dirty look, and then nodded.

"What a cute little group!" she said. "Follow me."

She led them down an aisle filled with various blue and gray uniforms, all hanging on racks. There were various sizes, and the choices seemed a bit overwhelming.

"Here," she said. "I assume y'all want to be Union troops?"

Kansas and Dusti nodded, and Gestalt shrugged.

"Okay. Here are three of our best uniforms. Each comes with a sword and a hat. The swords are fake, of course, but Jake's Civil War Replica's across the parking lot sells the real thing if you wish. Your whip is actually not completely out of period," she said, pointing to Kansas' hip. "So you can probably wear it with the uniform and not get too much slack."

"Thanks," he said. "That works for me."

The girl smiled. "There are dressing rooms at the back of the store, but if I didn't get your sizes right by guessing, come find me. I'll give you ten percent off."

"Can we just wear these out of here?" Dusti asked. "We are kind of late."

"Sure. You can just keep them on and come up to the register with the tags to check out. I'll keep an eye out for you, and get you going as quick as I can."

"Thanks."

They headed for the dressing rooms, and Dusti went into one marked ladies. Kansas pulled Gestalt to one side before he went in.

"Look, put on the uniform. Pull the hat down low, tight on your head. Don't look people in the eye on your way out."

"I want a sword," the creature said.

"You have one."

"A real one."

"Okay. After. For now, please just act as normal as you can."

"Fine," Gestalt said.

Kansas watched him go in to one of the makeshift booths, and entered one himself, changing as quickly as he could. He was the first to be done, so waited for the others. Gestalt was next, and he looked good, but unhappy. There was little Kansas could do to make that better in any way, so he didn't try.

Then Dusti emerged. She was beautiful, although the uniform hid her curves, it fit her thin body snugly, and she looked like a warrior, perhaps more than any of the rest of them. Her dark hair was hidden by the hat she wore, her green eyes stood out from the blue and gold of what was clearly an officer's uniform. The sword hung from her belt and followed the curve of her leg precisely.

He stared for a moment, and then her eyes met his. "That bad, huh?"

"Oh, no," he said. "You look great."

She snorted. "Sure."

"Believe me or not, you do." They walked toward the front of the store, and several men turned to stare at her. That made Kansas happy, not only that he was right about how she looked, but because it took attention away from the sullen Gestalt.

Their salesgirl spotted them, led them to a register, and gave them the promised discount even though everything fit perfectly.

"It's going to storm tonight," she said. "In fact, here are couple disposable ponchos on us. And do be careful. I assume you're going to the Cemetery or the Devil's Den?"

Kansas watched Gestalt for a reaction. At the mention of the Devil's Den, he stiffened.

That's it, he thought. Gotcha.

Out loud he said, "Yes. We'll be at Devil's Den tonight."

"Well, I'll be around. I might see you."

Kansas grinned, but he wondered if Cthulhu or Gestalt had taken into account a battle reenactment going on tonight.

It seemed that might add some excitement to their adventure.

THIRTEEN

Preparing to Prepare

"You can't do this tonight, Cthulhu." Davey Jones put his hands on his hips, or what was left of them. He was a round man in nearly every sense of the word. His face topped a round chest that descended into an even rounder belly. His shoulders were rounded from poor posture. His legs were thick and round, his knees barely visible, his feet round platforms that seemed too small for his bulk, and his arms were short, round appendages that looked as if they would strain to reach his knees let alone far enough to tie his shoes.

Which was not a problem, since he was wearing flip flops over socks, a look not common to this part of the world.

They stood in an odd room on the bottom floor of a three story structure. Form the outside, it looked like a home, but this room held rows of dark gray chairs on an equally gray floor. The walls were black, and at the front of the room opposite the door was what appeared to be a stage.

The room was lit by LED torches, but ones that flickered and were clearly dimmed. There were spotlights on a track above, but they were currently not lit.

"We have to do it tonight. I am being pursued."

"By?"

"Gestalt. And a human bounty hunter named Kansas. He has some woman with him, too."

"It doesn't help that you have almost half the country crying out for you to run for president."

Cthulhu smiled. "I know, but it is kinda great, you know?"

"Yeah, yeah. But you don't understand. Tonight I have a big tour of the Devil's Den, and there will be a reenactment happening at the same time."

"So?"

"So? Do you want to summon the horseman with a whole crowd of people around?"

"Why will it matter?"

Davey hesitated. "Do you know why I have lasted here for so long, and kept my job, even though I am nearly as old as this battlefield and have been on earth nearly half the time since the fight occurred?"

"Well, because people come and go, you alter your appearance—"

"Yet never seem to age? That is getting harder to do in today's connected world."

"I get that, but you're a legend."

"A legend who does not mind being noticed and takes active steps to protect myself. The horseman, he doesn't share our love for the limelight."

"What are you saying?"

"If you summon him in front of a crowd, you may never get the treasure under that rock. He could seal it forever."

"But I have an agreement with him."

"An agreement that would likely be broken by your actions tonight."

"I can't—"

"There is a way," Karen said quietly. Cthulhu felt her look, and knew she was still angry with him, but he wanted to hear what she had to say. "If we do things right, we can make him appear to be part of the reenactment."

"And how would we do that?" Davey asked.

"Someone can complain about him not looking realistic."

"Ha! Who would do that?"

She simply pointed to herself. "No one will be surprised at me complaining. I'm Karen after all. I do have a reputation to uphold."

Davey looked her up and down. "You do look the type."

"What type would that be?" she snapped back.

He recoiled. "Sorry. I mean, I didn't mean to say you were any type. Not based on how you look or anything."

"See?" she said calmly. "I got you flustered, and you are a 400 year old—whatever you are. Imagine how the kids and their meek parents will feel when I speak up."

"They'll believe you."

"You can work with the horseman to save face, and then you can still get your treasure."

"The idea has merit," Davey said.

"Agreed," Cthulhu said. "That is a great idea."

Karen shot him dagger eyes but followed them with a smile.

"What did you do, Cthulhu?" Davey asked.

"He called me his queen. Like I was a possession," Karen answered. "And then let me know I could hold the position for a week, no more."

"That's awful," he said. "What happened to Idh-yaa, Cthulhu?"

"Divorce. The kids are grown, and apparently she has grown sick of my evil ways."

"When did you two meet?" he said, addressing them both.

"A couple days ago."

"And yet you already act like you've been married for a long time. You've totally skipped that initial sickening honeymoon phase."

"Not completely," Karen said.

Cthulhu blushed.

"Well, um, good then?" Davey said. "Why do the two of you want to fight? Do you want to throw a good thing like that away?"

"Well, no. Not really. I mean, we don't know what it is yet," Karen said.

"And you know they will make me go back," Cthulhu said. "I can't stay. Not for long."

"Well, you could remain," Davey said. "You could take on a life like mine."

"I would love to, if only it were that simple."

"It is. You know what you need to do."

Karen stared at him. "Is this true?"

"Sort of. There would be a—cost."

"Do you think I am worth that cost?"

Cthulhu looked down at his shoes, realizing how unnatural they looked on his feet. How unnatural the clothes he wore were to him and his kind. But he also relished in how great he felt.

He almost felt like he was glowing. He felt warm considering the possibilities.

"I think so," he said. "There are choices. You could come with me. If we stayed here, some things would change for me."

"But you could get a job, something like this, or even sailing tours."

"You have to be nice to humans all the time."

"Not always. You get a certain leeway here."

"Tell me about that."

"I am seen as an old guy. Grumpy is a part of the act. I can treat people poorly, and they think it is just my personality."

"Huh."

"I do what I want Cthulhu. You could too. There is something you can have here on earth you will not find in the land of the Great Old Ones."

"What is that?"

"Freedom."

"This is a great chat," Karen interrupted. "And I would love Cthulhu to stay. I am sure he and I will be talking more about it very soon. But the first thing we need to do is prepare for tonight. How are we going to join the reenactment?"

"Well, I may not be much in solving the problems of love," Davey said. "But this I can help with. Come with me."

He turned and led them to a small room behind the stage. The walls inside were black as well, but there were several rods with clothing hanging on them. It was all Civil War stuff, from farmers to soldiers, from nurses uniforms to formal dresses.

"You, Miss Karen—"

"Miz," she said. "Not Miss or Missus."

"Excuse me, Miss Karen," he said. "You will be a spectator. There were ladies and even occasionally gentlemen who would come out to watch the war. It will make a lot of sense then for you to complain."

"And me?" Cthulhu asked.

"Well, you my large and tentacle-faced friend, will play the role of the larger than life Lieutenant Charles E. Hazlett."

"Wasn't he killed?" Karen asked.

"Yes, but that will not happen tonight."

"Well, I know that."

"It will be a great disguise. I will help you remove the treasure. For a small token, of course."

"Of course," Cthulhu said. "Not a problem at all."

"Come back here by five to get ready. Before that, I have a suggestion for you."

"Yes?"

"Go back to your hotel. Rest. Eat. Hydrate. And talk out whatever the two of you have going on and decide what to do next."

"It's really none of your business," Karen told him.

"Miz Karen, you are absolutely right," he said. "But you two have an opportunity for a fine love story, one based on mutual hatred of nearly all other things besides each other. It is perhaps the greatest opportunity of all time. You may not be his, but you have forgotten a universal truth even a bachelor like me knows well."

"What is that?"

"What's his, is yours. That is the way relationships work. You could be a very rich woman."

He smiled, and Cthulhu shot him a dirty look. "We'll be back," was all he said. Karen led the way outside, and Cthulhu followed, feeling a bit like a small puppy.

THE TRIO EXITED the costume shop. Kansas felt ready, as if he were on the cusp of something great. Devil's Den. That is where they would find the treasure, and Cthulhu. And with that clue, that hint Gestalt has inadvertently shared with them, they didn't need him anymore. Not exactly.

That meant it was time for phase one of their plan. But losing Gestalt would not be easy at this time. Last time he'd hijacked a police cruiser, dispatched the officer, and managed to avoid easy detection to pull them over and join them again.

But why? What did he need from them besides the cover of traveling with humans? Transportation perhaps? But they were close enough to Gettysburg now he could get there on foot, or steal and take another car, nearly anything.

They didn't need them, and as far as Kansas could tell, he did not need them anymore either. So why did he stay? When he'd hijacked the police cruiser, why did he need them then?

There had to be a reason. Why did Cthulhu travel with Karen? Was it just about appearances, or was it about something else entirely?

He glanced at the creature from the corner of his eye, but the hat pulled low hid the creatures features and his eyes. He couldn't tell anything about what he was thinking.

He looked at Dusti, too, and sucked in a breath between his teeth. She was gorgeous and looked incredibly powerful. Once he looked her way, he could hardly tear his eyes away from her. It would be great to be able to talk things through with her, figure out next steps, but they would need to get rid of Gestalt first.

The answer rolled up in front of the store. A security guard, rolled slowly by in a car with lights similar to those of a police car, and the driver stared at the trio, his gaze seeming to focus on Gestalt, even though you couldn't really see much.

Couldn't really see much.

Kansas fake tripped over his own feet, and shoved Gestalt in the back. The creature tripped as well, and his hat flew from his head.

Kansas fell to one side, rolled onto his back, and watched the security guard react. His eyes widened, and he brought a radio to his mouth.

In less than a second Dusti was at Kansas' side. She grabbed his hand to help him up, but leaned in and whispered in his ear, "Good job."

She helped him to his feet, and then turned.

Gestalt was a quick thinker and a quick mover. He was up, his hat back on his head, and he seamlessly joined a group of men dressed as soldiers just exiting the store.

A moment later, and even Kansas couldn't pick him out from the crowd.

"Stop right there!" a voice came from a megaphone attached to the car. "Don't move."

The driver got out. He was tall, almost mountainous as mountain ranges in Pennsylvania went, and he was athletic, or at least used to be. A small gut betrayed what was probably a newly acquired taste for beer, and his poop-brown uniform clung tightly to his frame.

"Oh, thank God," Dusti said. "We were just going to call someone. Did you see that creature run off?"

"I did," he said suspiciously. "What was he doing with you?"

Kansas could see, actually feel, her turning on the charm. She entered damsel in distress mode, letting some of her confidence slide into her back pocket to be used later. Her hands came up, fluttering back and forth like scared birds or nervous butterflies.

And the new arrival bought it.

"It's okay. Calm down, ma'am. He's gone now. What did he want from you?"

"He made us take him in there," she pointed to the store. "He wanted a uniform. He said he was trying to catch Cthulhu?"

"Cthulhu? The monster for President everyone is saying is here for some reason? The creature who rarely visits earth?"

"Yeah. He said he is from his world. Named Gestalt."

"Does he look like this?" The guard opened his phone, and showed them the sketch from the news, the one provided by the police officer the night before.

"Yep, that's him," Dusti said.

"Do you agree, sir?" he asked Kansas.

"Absolutely. That's him."

"Damn. Okay, this is my lucky day. I need to call this in. Can I contact you if I need to?"

"Sure," Dusti said sweetly, and rattled off a number he wrote down.

"Thanks," he said. "You two take care and be careful of that thing. I hear he is dangerous."

"Will do."

With that declaration, he turned and left.

"What number did you give him?" Kansas asked. Her confidence was back on, the damsel in distress mask discarded, but kept safely in case of emergency.

"That was my number when I was a kid. I have no idea who has the number now."

"Ha! Good one."

"Good call taking him out, too. I was thinking about how to make that happen at the same time you were."

"Well, we got lucky. But before he circles back around or the guard does, let's get the hell out of here."

"Absolutely. Where to?"

"Let's go to the store, and then we can head to the hotel and catch a nap. I have a feeling it is going to be a late night," Dusti said.

"Me too. And we will need snacks for a stakeout. You can't have a stakeout without snacks."

They jumped in the truck, did an internet search for groceries near them, and headed out.

In the mirror, Kansas thought he saw one of the soldiers separate from the group in the parking lot and stare after them. He wasn't sure if it was Gestalt or not, but he wasn't going to wait to find out.

After a quick shopping trip that involved the acquisition of a cart full of pistachios, potato chips, and energy drinks, they headed back to their hotel.

Most of the snacks they left in the truck, and they headed upstairs. Dusti followed right behind Kansas.

He swiped his card for his room and turned to tell her he would see her later after they took and nap and found her still standing there.

"Can I just nap in your room, too?" she asked.

"I-uh-sure," he said.

"I just don't want to be alone right now."

They went inside, and Kansas looked awkwardly at the bed.

"Don't worry," she said. "We can share. Just stay on your side," she said.

He was suddenly glad he'd opted for a king bed. He lay down on the side nearest the door, and she lay on the side nearest the small window.

She turned away from him and fell asleep in seconds. Tiny, cute snores came from her side of the bed.

Kansas lay on his back, his hands moving around. He was unsure where to put them, how to sleep with someone so gorgeous next to him. Eventually he turned away from her and drifted into dream-filled sleep. He dreamed a Devil was chasing him, a large serpent, a treasure chest mounted to its back. The dream ended when its giant mouth opened to swallow him whole, and he ducked deeper inside the creature.

At that moment, he fell into a deep sleep, and the next sound he heard was the loud blaring of an alarm.

FOURTEEN

Haunting and Haunted

The adequate hotel room had a bed, a desk of sorts, a small dining table, and the bathroom. There was a tiny luggage/closet area, and it had been overrun by Karen's things. That was fine. Cthulhu had little he hadn't purchased along the way, and he didn't really need to hang any of it up.

He looked forward to tonight, but between now and then was the chasm of this conversation, opened like many portals both of old worlds and new ones. They were activated by a male of nearly any species opening his mouth wide and inserting his foot. The depth and width of the chasm, and the size of the portal threatening to suck him into a relationship free existence depended entirely on how deep the foot had gone.

A famous philosopher of the Great Old Ones once said, "Man who put foot in mouth get athlete's tongue." Cthulhu had never found a statement so true as that one in this moment. His tongue and even his throat burned and itched.

For this affliction, there was only one cure. The dreaded "talking things out."

Cthulhu sat at the desk in an awkward and uncomfortable chair that swiveled and was really too tall to fit under the surface. He pulled out the center drawer, and closed it, noting there was a lock mechanism of some sort. He looked at it, on one side and on the other, then leaned down to see what it might lock into.

He couldn't for the life of him figure out how this would work, what one would lock or unlock it with, and how this small piece of metal could possibly secure what one might put in the drawer.

And what would one put in there? What occupant of a hotel room would have something remotely valuable enough to secure in a desk drawer, but not possessing enough value to belong in the safe?

"Are you done staring at that thing?" Karen asked.

He reluctantly turned to look at her. "I-sure. I just can't figure out how—"

She waved her hand and he stopped speaking. "Listen, we need to get some things out in the open," she said. "You're here on vacation, right?"

He nodded. *Answer yes or no questions,* he thought. *Stay in the safe zone.*

"So what am I? Just some kind of fling?"

He shook his head.

"So what am I?"

Uh-oh. Choose your words carefully.

"I -I didn't expect you. I mean, why are you here? Are you on vacation?"

"Yes, but we're not talking about me. We're talking about you."

"Uh, okay."

"So?"

"I never intended to have a fling or anything else. I like you, and I recognize a kindred spirit in you."

"Kindred spirit?" Her eyes gleamed with a kind of humor, but "be careful where you go" look.

It was one he knew well after centuries of marriage.

"Yes. A similar evil with disdain for pretty much everyone and everything."

"And?"

"Well, I like that. It makes me feel good. I've never met anyone quite like you. I may be a little more evil than you, and I think of consequences differently."

"For example?"

"I wanted to end the Lenny's manager!" he shouted, then stopped himself. "You were just content with a gift card," he said more calmly.

"Yes. But what do you think having to give me that gift card did to the rest of his day, let alone his week? He likely traumatized his employees. His level customer service probably went off the charts for the rest of the day. He may turn around his attitude for a week, a month, even forever. Or he may quit his job and go on to something else. I've seen it happen before."

"What's your point?"

"Ending him, as you say, would have been a mercy. I have started a cycle of suffering not only for him, but one he will pass on to others."

"Wow." Cthulhu looked at his hands, and then went to slide the desk drawer out as a distraction. It was stuck, and he couldn't get it open.

"Do you see?" she said. "We are on the same level."

"I suppose we are. But I don't know where to go from here?"

"Where do you want to go from here?"

"I would love—" he stopped short. If he said what he wanted to say, she would likely never speak to him again. "I want to get to know you better," he said. "For longer than a week would allow. A month feels like it would not be enough time."

"So? What should we do about that?"

"Well, we are constrained. We are from different worlds. Each of us must go home at some point, or one must go home with the other."

"You could stay here."

"I could, yes. Probably for a long time. But I would eventually have to leave."

"Your friend Davey does not have to leave."

"Oh, but he will eventually. Or he will have to move. His long life will become suspect if it has not already, especially in these digital times. It used to be easy to fake documents. Things have gotten harder."

"Perhaps."

"And people know more about me and my kind. Your fiction writers opened their minds and now that we are here, it is harder than ever to hide."

"Harder, but not impossible."

"You could come home with me."

"True. Although I know nothing of your world, and I have a feeling I would not be accepted."

"It has been done."

"With what result?"

Cthulhu thought about it. *Without good results,* he realized. *Nothing good had ever come from a human in the world of the Great Old Ones.*

"Not good," he mumbled.

"What did you say?"

"Not good," he said, looking her in the eyes and speaking more clearly. "But it could, with you. You're different."

"That is the truest thing you have said. And you are right, it could work. And so could you staying here. There are no guarantees regarding either choice."

"There are never guarantees with love."

"Love?" she asked.

"Love," he stated. "I know it has only been a couple of days. But I think I love you. I think we could work well together."

"Me, too."

"What?" Cthulhu swallowed, hard.

"Me, too. I like you a lot. More than I probably should. So what do we do about it?"

155

"Let's get through tonight. Get the treasure, the first of many to be honest," he said. "We could be the most chaotic team of all time."

"We could," she said. "With your resources and me being— well, me— we could change the world."

"I promise I will think about your world."

"I, too, will think about yours."

She moved towards him, and Cthulhu moved to stand and embrace her. The desk drawer caught on his pants pocket, and he yanked at it. It wouldn't budge.

"Argh!" he roared, and readied to rip it from its place in the desk.

"Allow me," Karen said. She took a nail file from her pocket, worked it into the gap between the desk top and the drawer, and slid it to one side.

The drawer unlocked and slid free. Cthulhu freed it from his pants pocket and stood.

They embraced. Then kissed. Then moved toward the bed, clothes falling to the floor piece by piece.

An hour later, he awoke to a blaring alarm.

AT FIRST, Kansas thought the alarm was coming from inside the room. He tried to move, but something was across him.

An arm. And a leg. And something was pressed against his back.

Not something. Someone.

"Dusti," he said. "You realize you're holding my hand?"

He felt it. Something. A tiny pressure on his left buttock, the one facing the ceiling.

"Am I?" she said. "What's that noise?"

"Some kind of alarm. Where is your other hand?"

"On top of one of the bed pillows."

"That's not a pillow."

"Ah!" she said, snatching her hand away. Kansas rolled to his feet.

On the other side of the bed, Dusti did the same.

"So, an alarm. Is that coming from outside? I wonder what that means?"

"The news!" He said, snatching the remote form the table. He turned on the television. "The news will know what is happening."

"Yes!" Dusti said. Her voice was much too enthusiastic for the circumstance, but he kind of understood.

Had they been accidentally cuddling? Or had it been purposeful?

He stretched, twirling his arms around and stretching first one shoulder than another.

"Some nap, huh?"

"Yeah. Yeah. Helluva nap!" she said.

The television came to life, but there was no news, only an afternoon soap opera.

He looked out the window toward the street, but there was no panic. No one was moving in the streets except for a few soldiers dressed in Civil War garb, marching in time.

The alarm stopped as soon as it had started. It was just marking the start of the reenactment.

That made total sense now that he saw it.

He turned around and found Dusti right behind him, really only inches away.

"What is it?" she asked.

"The reenactment is starting. What time is it?"

She glanced around. The clock on the hotel nightstand flashed 12:00 over and over like it had been unplugged or had lost power.

She reached in her pocket and pulled out her phone. They were still close, and Kansas had no idea how to cure that situation. His heartbeat sped up, and he struggled to keep his breathing under control. She filled his senses. Her smell, the sight of her face and the depth of her eyes. He fell into them, diving as far as he could. Her presence consumed him.

"It's five," she said, sliding the phone back into one of the pockets in her uniform. She had taken off the jacket at some point, and he wished she had it back on, to shield him from the heat radiating from her skin.

She looked into his eyes. He couldn't pull his gaze away.

"I suppose we should get out there soon," he said. "Although Cthulhu probably won't show until after dark."

"Right, but we don't know. We should be ready."

"Right," he said, moving his face closer to hers. "We shouldn't waste a bit of time."

"Yes," she said. "We should hurry." She turned her head and brought her lips closer to his. He leaned forward until they met.

The initial awkwardness of a first kiss faded into dancing tongues, and roaming hands. He slid his arms around her, lowered his hand to the small of her back and pulled her close.

She broke the kiss to gasp, and then resumed, her hands now around his neck. She slipped one hand down to his chest, and rubbed it up and down, spreading warmth throughout his body.

He moved his hands from the small of her back to her hips, and then ran one hand up under her shirt.

She gasped again. "No."

"No?" he said, pausing.

"No, not now. We need to stay focused."

"Not now?" he said, slowing his mind down, and slowly untangling from her.

She gently pushed him away. "It's not that I don't want to, Kansas. Because I do. I really do."

"Good. Me, too," he said, then realized how stupid that sounded.

"But right now, Cthulhu is out there. He's planning to get his treasure tonight, and if he does, and gets away, or if Gestalt catches him first, all our work the last couple of days will be for nothing."

She was right, of course. Kansas took a deep breath. She took a step back from him, leaned in and kissed him with her mouth slightly open. It was a promise of more to come later.

He smiled. "Okay. You're right. And it's time for phase two of my plan."

"Phase two?"

"Getting rid of Gestalt was just the beginning. The second is to alert people to the fact that Cthulhu is here. At just the right moment, we will alert them to exactly where he is, and then the crowd will control him for us."

"Are you sure that will work?"

"It will," he said. "Because it has to. Either they will surround and overwhelm him, or Gestalt will take him away. We'll be left with the treasure, and we win."

"How do we start that?"

"Are you on Twitter?" he asked.

"Am I?" she said. She opened the app on her phone and turned it toward him. The Black Widow had over 17,000 followers.

He grinned and went to the nightstand and grabbed his own phone. He showed her his only slightly larger following.

"Now what?"

"Look at trending topics near me."

Top of the list was #Cthulhu2024 and #CthulhuinDelaware. She smiled at him.

"So we use those two hashtags," he said. "And we add one more of our own."

He typed a Tweet and showed it to her.

"Where did Cthulhu go?" it read. "#Cthulhu2024 #CthulhuinDelaware #CthulhuinGettysburg."

She grinned, typed a similar Tweet, and hit send.

Immediately notifications, replies, retweets, and likes showed up. The new hashtag took on a life of its own within minutes.

They both added a couple of Tweets, and then looked at each other.

"I need to get straightened up a bit," she said, grabbing her costume top. "Then we can go."

Kansas nodded. "Me too. You go first. This is going to be fun."

"Yes, yes it is," she said, and disappeared into the bathroom.

While he waited for her, he continued to watch Twitter explode.

Then he saw a tweet while he was strolling through. ".@Gestalt may have failed @Cthulhu, but we are coming for you." The name on the account was simple and straightforward. @TheGreatOldOnes.

He smiled, but something deep inside was uncomfortable with the news, and he shivered.

"We are coming for you," he read again.

He may have started something bigger than he intended, something out of this world.

A few moments later, Dusti came out of the bathroom, and he traded her places.

But the message was never far from his mind.

When he finished washing his face and brushing his teeth, he picked up his phone again, this time to see a more specific and haunting notification.

"@KansasSmith, @TheGreatOldOnes followed you."

He shuddered, closed the app, and put his phone in his pocket before stepping out of the bathroom.

Dusti was there, face pale, staring at her phone, and looked up at him.

"You have to see this," she said, turning the phone toward him.

"Direct message from @TheGreatOldOnes," it said.

"Have you read it yet?"

She shook her head.

"Open it."

She did, and her hands shook as she read it. She turned it so he could see it too, and he put his arm around her.

"We want Cthulhu and Gestalt," it said. "We will trade. Your souls and your freedom for their location. Now."

"How do I reply?" she asked.

"Don't," Kansas said. "Close the app. Let's go. We'll worry about them later."

But as much as he wanted to reassure her, he was worried about them right now.

FIFTEEN

Going Social

"What is that?" Karen asked from the bed. The blanket covered her mostly naked body but fell away partially as she sat up.

Cthulhu smiled at her and moved to the window. He saw a unit of soldiers marching in unison.

"It's time," he said. "The reenactment is beginning."

"Already?"

"Yes. We need to get to Davey's place and get ready. We won't be ready for the treasure until nightfall, but we should join the army early to avoid suspicion."

"Okay," she said. "I am really excited."

"Me, too," he said. He was, but an underlying fear had him both anxious and puzzled. He had no idea why he felt this way, but there was almost a presence he could feel.

"I'm going to get ready," he said, gathered a new set of clothes and went into the bathroom. It consisted of a pair of khakis, a simple polo shirt, and he thought would go well with the shoes they'd purchase. He washed his face, paying special attention to the spaces between the tentacles there, and brushed his teeth. Once he was dressed, he checked his image in the harshly lit mirror. He looked almost normal, and definitely not threatening. He adjusted his collar and walked out of the bathroom.

Karen was seated on the side of the bed. The alarm had stopped blaring, and things were quiet.

She looked up at him, her face pale. "Do you have a Twitter?"

"Doesn't everyone?"

"Well, yes, but—"

"What?" he said.

She turned the screen of her phone toward him. Trending topics were on the right side of the near-notebook sized screen. Top of the list was a new one. #CthulhuinGettysburg.

Under it was #Cthulhu2024 and #CthuolhluinDelaware.

In her feed was the top tweet in the first hashtag.

It was from @KansasSmith. "Where did Cthulhu go?" it said, followed by all three hashtags.

Cthulhu roared, and someone in the room next to them banged on the wall.

"I told them no neighbors," Karen said.

"Well, they probably got busy with the reenactment," he said.

"Still, I am going to complain."

"Not now. We have to go."

She gave him a stare, but Cthulhu just looked back at her. She dropped her eyes.

"You're right. But I will let management know later."

"Good," he said. "I approve."

"My turn to get ready," she said. She let the blanket fall, gathered her clothes, and walked naked into the bathroom. He watched her go, and then turned his attention to his phone and his Twitter feed.

The hashtags were blowing up, and then he saw a mention. He clicked on it.

".@Gestalt may have failed, but @Cthulhu we are coming for you." The user was @TheGreatOldOnes.

Cthulhu knew who ran that account, who monitored it, and who would be looking for him. He got a chill.

He reached around in his bag and found a yellow kerchief. He tied it across his nose and mouth and looked in the mirror over the desk. It hid his face, not perfectly, but what would have to do.

All he needed was a couple of hours, and then he could be home free. No matter who the Great Old Ones sent, he could defeat them, but if they sent more than one soldier...

He would need help to defeat them, and as powerful as Karen had proved to be, it might not be enough. And Davey would not stand with him too strongly. He would help behind the scenes, but he wouldn't risk being pulled from his life here back into the underworld.

They would be on their own. They would have to be both clever and fast.

Then an idea came to him.

An evil, awful, and most excellent idea to turn things around on his enemies. All of them.

He typed a Tweet and hit send.

Two could play at that game.

Karen came out, fully dressed and ready. Getting to Davey's was the first order of business.

He hoped she would not look too closely at Twitter and see his message. He needed her to be surprised too.

She looked at the kerchief with a puzzled expression on her face. "What's that about?"

He carefully showed her the thread on Twitter.

"Damn," she said. "We'll have to be careful and keep you disguised well."

Karen kissed him on the cheek, and even through the bandana he felt the heat from her mouth and breath warm his body. He was in love despite himself.

That felt just fine. A new wave of confidence in Karen, his plan, and the future events of the evening swelled inside and through him.

They were going to do this and get away from his treasure. Then he knew of a place, a place mostly unknown and not often visited where they could go and spend time together.

And determine what the future looked like. Because he wanted to figure out how to work it out. This world had become crowded, stuffy, and full of evil and division. Maybe he could find a way to stay here after all.

They went downstairs and headed for Davey's home. They parked several streets away.

"Just in case," he told Karen. "We don't need to telegraph where we are and who we are consulting with."

It was true. The vehicle was recognizable, and so was Cthulhu, but the bandana helped. Almost no one looked twice at him as they walked down the street.

At Davey Jones's door, they knocked and heard a "Come in!"

Cthulhu pushed the door open with caution and Karen followed. Near the odd stage in the living area were two costumes hanging on a portable rod.

Davey had picked well. He likely had a Twitter, too, and had discovered what was going on, because Cthulhu's costume was elaborate, with a huge hat, a bandana that was more period, and a large sword.

Cthulhu's breath caught when he saw it, and his side ached in sympathy.

He remembered the feeling of it entering his flesh, remembered swiping at the man who had stabbed him, sending him into the sea.

Finally came the healing process. The sword had been coated in a poison dangerous to his kind, supplied by Elhort.

No matter what his form, he could still feel the scar, stretching and molding with him.

Sending Gestalt back to the realm of the old ones using that sword and killing those who stood in his way would be even greater. He could almost picture it entering Kansas' side.

He clapped his hands together, and then turned his attention to Karen's costume. It was gorgeous.

Davey had chosen one from his stash that would fit her well. There was a parasol that matched the white lace trimmings on the dress. It was high-necked, cinched at the waist with a long skirt. There were boots that would hardly show but looked both comfortable and fetching.

On the stage beside it was a bag for her to carry, more of a square box, but with straps and a latch to hold it closed.

Cthulhu looked up questioningly. Davey smiled. "There are some useful, more modern things inside, including a ecto-plasm detector and a small pistol. And the parasol? Ma'am, will you come here please?"

He turned to Karen who just stared and moved forward. Her mouth was open in awe, and she didn't even correct his anti-quated use of the word ma'am. Slowly she approached and he handed her the small, almost transparent umbrella.

"Push this switch on the handle to open it," Davey said.

She took it from his hand and complied. It popped open into something that would clearly not block the sun well, and of course wouldn't be necessary tonight, but she spun it anyway, then closed it.

"Now, hit the switch next to it," he said.

She did, and then gasped as a long blade appeared from the end of it. It was double edged, long and deadly looking.

"Just in case," Davey said. He glanced at Cthulhu and smiled. Karen just stared at the outfit.

"Is there somewhere I can get changed?" she asked.

"Sure," Davey said, showing her to a back room opposite the costume area they had seen earlier.

When they were alone, Cthulhu shed his normal looking clothes and got into costume. Davey helped him with the sword.

"Thanks for this," Cthulhu said, touching the hilt.

"I knew you would love it," Davey said. "I'll be right back."

Cthulhu stood, thinking, wondering if his plan would work. This social media thing was new, and he never knew how those of this world would react to it.

A moment later, Karen walked out from where she'd been getting changed, and Cthulhu's breath caught in his throat. The dress was perfect. Her broad shoulders filled it nicely, her breasts were prominent but not overly so, and the dress clung nicely to her generous waist. It fell over hips and stopped just above the floor. She twirled.

"This is so fantastic," she said. She pushed the button on the parasol, and the blade emerged. She parried, and spun, and thrust with the sword, and stopped.

Davey walked out from the other side of the stage. He wore a Union uniform, an eye patch, and a large hat with a giant feather. It was outlandish and amazing.

His round body looked oddly contained by all the cloth. He managed to look regal, fierce, and deadly, things Cthulhu knew he could be if he wanted to.

"I'll lead a tour this way," he said. "It will be a great distraction. Is everyone ready to go?"

Cthulhu smiled, and then his evil grin got even wider. He looked from Karen to his friend, and back again.

"Let's do this thing," he said.

"READY?" Kansas asked.

They were parked in downtown Gettysburg, in a "lot" that was really a dirt area behind an old home, probably a period one. The "parking spot" had cost them fifteen bucks, but they needed something like it. They needed to look normal, and blend in.

"Sure," she said, clearly nervous.

They knew how dangerous Gestalt could potentially be, and he was likely not on their side anymore, if he ever had been. Even though they had the same goals, the creature had ditched them as soon as he'd gotten what he needed, a group of humans to blend in with.

That was fine, because they wanted him gone anyway now that they didn't need him anymore either.

But Kansas had felt a bit more comfortable knowing what the creature was up to and keeping an eye on him.

Now others of the Great Old Ones were coming, and they knew who they were, and even where they were.

There were a lot of things going on, and they would need to be extremely watchful and careful.

"Okay, let's go," he said. He slid from the passenger side of the truck, and she slid out the driver's door. He grabbed their bags of snacks and a picnic basket. They turned to look around them.

At least they fit in. Nearly everyone was in either a Union or Confederate uniform of some sort. The mix of cars in the lot was odd to say the least. There were older Hondas, Toyotas, and Chevys. There were several Mercedes. Only a few trucks were here and there.

Costumes varied from elaborate too clearly homemade. They were a distance from the Gettysburg Museum and gift shop, and even slightly further from their destination of the Devil's Den.

There were a variety of weapons present. Some looked like actual period muskets, and others were clearly replicas. Most men wore swords, and there were several women in various uniforms as well.

As they walked along, they also saw several women in formal dresses, dressed as the women of the time who watched the battles like they were a spectator sport. Some were accompanied by men dressed in tuxedos and others walked with men in uniform. Nearly everyone carried either some kind of bags filled with food and drinks, or large, wicker picnic baskets likely filled to overflowing.

There was an excited chatter in the crowd. Everyone seemed to have one thing in common, and that was a love for the history of this place and this time.

The air was hot and humid, but most seemed not to notice. There were umbrellas, some folded ponchos under arms, but for the most part the crowd marched toward the battlefield and the storm with little concern.

Many Civil War battles were fought in inclement weather. Why should this reenactment be exempt? Kansas thought. Besides that, it meant great cover for them, but also for the Great Old Ones, Cthulhu, and Gestalt.

He felt electricity all around them, and not just from the threat of lightning. Something big would happen tonight, one way or the other.

They moved with the crowd. No one seemed to be going the opposite direction. In this section of town, there were no cars on the streets, at least not at the moment. He hadn't seen barriers, but either they were in place, or the locals and others simply knew this space would be occupied by reenactors for the evening.

They reached a grassy area and began a gentle climb up a paved path. There were others around them, walking up the grassy area, and there were a few uniformed park rangers from time to time directing people and handing out some sort of program.

Kansas took one and glanced it over. He checked his watch. The official battle reenactment would start at eight, just before the sun would set and it would get dark.

It was just after six. They had a couple of hours to go.

Cthulhu would not make his move until after dark, likely in the heat of the "battle." The same would likely be true of The Great Old Ones, and Gestalt would either join with them or help them in some way.

That meant either they had to wait and react or be proactive and try to act ahead of time.

Cthulhu should be easy to pick out of the crowd. So should Gestalt.

They could follow them, he could time his Tweet perfectly for when they knew where the treasure was, let the crowd take care of their two primary opponents, then take the treasure and run.

And the Great Old Ones? Well, they were a wildcard to be dealt with when the time came.

They got to an open area next to a large rock formation. The Devil's Den. Several groups sat down, spreading blankets and opening picnic baskets.

"What now?" Dusti asked.

"Let's get closer to the rocks. That's likely where Cthulhu will be, and once we spot him, we can decide where to go from there."

"In the meantime?"

He held up the bags of snacks. "We feast! This is a stakeout, after all."

She smiled at him, and he offered his hand. She took it, and he imagined they looked like many of the other couples in the area. They selected a spot near a cut in the rocks and sat there.

The sun was still shining, but it struggled to push through the growing clouds. As they sat down, the clouds won their battle, and the temperature dropped a quick ten degrees.

Dusti shivered.

"You okay?" Kansas asked her.

"Yeah. I just felt something odd."

"It's just the clouds," he said, pointing up. But he felt it too. An unnatural cold that he couldn't tie just to the weather.

Something or somethings were here, and they were not friendly.

Evil had shown up with the disappearance of the sun, and in spite of the fact they were in the middle of a large crowd, he felt extremely exposed.

He opened a bag of chips, passed some to Dusti, and started to eat. But he didn't stop studying those around him.

As he grabbed another handful, a large droplet landed on his head followed by a second, and a third.

The rain had started early.

There were some canopies set up near the trees surrounding the grassy area, and several museum officials and others struggled to set up more.

"Come on," he told Dusti, who had started to pack up their food. "Let's take shelter."

But instead of heading for the trees with everyone else, he headed for the rock formation. He was betting there would be a place to take shelter there, watch, and wait.

They managed to squeeze under an overhang of rock before the sky really opened up. Rivulets of water ran down the rocks around them, quickly forming puddles just outside their place of shelter.

He heard a crunching sound behind him and turned.

Dusti had a handful of chips and was going to town on them.

"What?" She said. "We might as well eat while we wait."

He smiled. "You're absolutely right." He grabbed a piece of beef jerky and bit into it. "This isn't bad at all."

She passed him a plastic water bottle and he took a huge swig.

Lightning struck nearby, followed rapidly by a clap of thunder.

He stared.

In the flash of light, he'd seen a trio of figures moving toward the rocks. One soldier wore an eye patch, the other a bandana over his face. A woman was with them, dressed in a period dress and looking stunning. In the flash, he couldn't see any faces.

But they were headed directly towards them.

"This might be trouble," he told Dusti.

But she was already moving, preparing to move. She put their bags of food behind a rock and stood next to him.

"Who do you think they are?" she asked.

"I'm not sure," he said. But in the back of his mind, he was. He shivered with more than just the temperature and rain. The group was either emissaries of the Great Old Ones, or it was Cthulhu, Karen, and someone new.

Either way, evil was headed their way, and they had no way out.

He looked around form something, anything, that might give him a clue what to do.

Then he saw it. There was an opening, barely man sized, near the back of the cut they were in.

He moved towards it, and then heard a sound inside. It was like someone wailing in pain.

For a moment, he was transfixed, but another flash of lightning showed the trio of new arrivals even closer.

"Quick," he said. "Get inside." He pointed to the crevasse.

Dusti's face was pale, but she nodded. He went around her and squeezed in first. She was right behind him.

The air inside was shockingly cold, and the fury of the storm seemed to disappear. The air felt heavy, tainted.

The cave beyond the crevasse was much larger than he'd anticipated, and a moment after they entered, he heard it.

The sound of hoofbeats, far away at first, but coming closer.

He looked around. There was no place to hide.

"Run!" he said. He took Dusti's hand and pulled her the opposite direction of the hoofbeats.

But she quickly dropped his hand, and they both ran, the sound of a new danger echoing around them.

SIXTEEN

Back, Back, Back to the Wall

As the rain started the crowd dispersed, heading for tents set up by the woods and out of the rain.

That was perfectly fine with Cthulhu, and he could understand. Some of those costumes were expensive, and it would not do to get them wet and ruin them. Same with the weapons.

But ahead, he could see the entrance to the crevasse, the place where his treasure was hidden. It was early, early for the horseman, early even for them, but they could wait outside the cavern, in the shelter of the rocks. The cover of the storm created the perfect opportunity.

Lightning flashed, and thunder sounded almost immediately. He felt rather than saw Karen jump by his side, but she grabbed his hand, which seemed to calm her.

He strode forward, knowing Davey would not be far behind. Then lightning flashed again, and he saw it.

Someone was in the crevasse, or the area leading to it at least. Two someones, maybe three.

It couldn't be Kansas could it?

Not unless Gestalt had somehow tipped them off. Was the creature still with them.

He doubled his speed, and Karen stumbled before finding her feet and catching up with him. He wondered if Davey had seen what he had, and turned, finding his friend had fallen behind. He gestured to him and pointed, and Davey waved him on.

Cthulhu squinted. Lightning struck again, and he could see there were only two figures present, but he saw them head toward the cave entrance. They must have spotted it.

Good. The horseman would take care of them, and they would make a proper sacrifice.

But where—

Karen stumbled with a cry, and went down, nearly face first in a puddle, and Cthulhu turned to help her up.

"Watch out!" he heard Davey's faint cry over the noise of the storm, seeing what he said as much as hearing it. Then something struck him hard on his left side, and he hit the ground with whatever it was rolling on top of him.

At first, he thought it was a human soldier. He glimpsed a Union uniform, one with what had been gold accents, and he felt soaked wool against him as he struggled to push the figure off and away.

But the creature was strong, and then the smell reached his nostrils.

Gestalt.

He shoved harder, and managed to roll to his feet, only to find the other creature facing him.

Rain fell in sheets between them. Lightning struck again. So did Gestalt.

But this time Cthulhu was ready. He dodged the attack, shoving Gestalt as he went by, putting extra thrust behind a shove, and trying to trip him.

But his opponent went with the fall, tucking his shoulder and rolling to his feet. He rushed Cthulhu again, grinning. Cthulhu rushed to meet him and tripped.

He tried to catch himself, roll gracefully as Gestalt had done, but he failed. Instead he landed awkwardly on one shoulder, his arm folding under him, and his face landing in deep mud. He tried to breathe and got a mouthful of earth.

He turned in time to see Gestalt raise his giant arm, preparing to swing.

Lightning struck again, and Cthulhu rolled away just in time. The blow struck empty earth where his head had been. He found his feet and approached carefully. He stepped forward and nearly tripped again, finding there was a large spider at his feet, running between them and spinning a web.

He roared. The arm of his uniform split at the elbow as he raised his arm, and swung, destroying the web and sending the spider flying toward Gestalt's head.

The creature reached out deftly, caught the spider, and Cthulhu watched as it merged into his hand, becoming one with his skin. That stopped him, but only for a second.

He knew Gestalt's power, but he could command the water, bend it. The sea was his home, a storm often his tool.

He spun his finger over his head, creating a spinning whirlwind. It headed straight for Gestalt, but the creature was faster than he expected. He spun out of the way, reached for the ground, and pulled Karen to her feet.

Gestalt held her next to him, one hand tangled in her short hair, the other approaching her throat.

A spider crawled over his fingers, in and out.

"Come with me, and I let her go," Gestalt growled. "Don't, and I will take her with me instead."

Karen's eyes were wide, but not in fear. Cthulhu could see she was angry. She would be looking for a way to get away from her captor, escape, exact some sort of revenge, this time far beyond a complaint to the manager.

He smiled inside but did not let it show. Instead he put his hands in the air.

Behind Gestalt, he could see Davey approaching carefully.

He hoped the rain was hiding the battle. He hoped there were no more emissaries of the Great Old Ones here, not yet. Or that if they were, they would not find them.

Not now.

With his hands still raised, he put his fingers down into fists, twice, and then raised them again, hoping Davey would understand.

He saw that he did.

"Let her go," he said. "Take me. Tell the Great Old Ones you have me and leave her alone."

Gestalt grinned. "You are making the right choice. Come closer. Once I have you, I will let her go. Not before."

Davey was in place.

Cthulhu moved forward slowly until he was very close to the creature. He held out his hands.

Gestalt released Karen and moved to grab his wrists. Cthulhu shoved him with a roar and every bit of strength he had.

Gestalt went up and over Davey, who was kneeling behind him. He landed in the mud with a roar. Cthulhu leapt over his friend and went after him.

But Karen got there first. She pressed the hidden button on the Parasol. The blade shot out and she shoved it into Gestalt's throat.

Several small to medium sized spiders spilled out. The creature grabbed for his throat and gasped for breath he would not find.

Gestalt would not die from the wound, but Cthulhu knew what would end the emissary of Eihort. He drew the sword Davey had given him, and raised it, before he felt a hand on his shoulder.

It was Davey. His elegant hat with the feather was soaked through. His hair hung below it into his eyes. His eyes were narrow, and his mouth opened and closed, gathering breath the best he could.

With effort, he took two deep gulps of air.

"Don't," he said. "You can't."

"Why?"

"Do you want to stay here?"

"Yes."

"If you do this, Eihort will never stop hunting you. Show mercy. Simply send him home."

Cthulhu looked at Gestalt, whose throat was slowly healing.

"Go," he said. "Call off the Great Old Ones and go. Either that or die here."

Gestalt looked right and left, and then his eyes met Cthulhu's.

He grinned, shot to his feet and turned for Karen.

She was several feet away, covered in mud. The parasol dangled by her side, and her eyes were wide with shock. Gestalt sprinted toward her.

Cthulhu reacted. He took two long running steps after the creature and swung the sword.

He felt the impact, barely felt the vibration through his arms, and then saw Gestalt's head separate from his body. In delightful horror, it flew into the air, headed for the rocks. The now headless body collapsed forward, disintegrating into a host of spiders.

That got Karen moving. She stabbed the ones that ran for her with the blade on her parasol, doing so without mercy or compassion.

Cthulhu got those that moved slower, and a few moments later, they, and the body of Gestalt, were gone.

Davey ran up behind them.

"Now you did it," he said. "You'll never be able to rest again."

"Yes, I will," said Cthulhu. "I have a plan."

From the corner of his eye he saw Karen, now pale and wide eyed again. She swayed on her feet for a moment, and then her knees folded.

He managed to catch her before she hit the ground.

"Let's get her to shelter," Davey said. "Then I want to hear about this plan of yours."

They headed to the gash in the Devil's Den, Cthulhu carrying Karen.

Even her unconscious form was beautiful to him. He would do anything to protect her. Even betray his own kind if he had to.

Even if his plan worked, he might never be able to return to the land of the Great Old Ones. And he felt perfectly okay with that.

THE AIR RACED in and out of his lungs, and Kansas could never seem to get enough. There were tunnels under the Devil's Den, a maze, and the hoofbeats felt like they were coming from everywhere around them at once.

Every few seconds, he checked to see that Dusti was still with him. She seemed to be keeping up but seemed pretty exhausted too. He had no idea how long they would be able to keep this up. But he felt like hiding would not be an option. They were in the home of this creature, and it held all the cards. It would know where they were, chase them down, find them, no matter where they were. The only hope was to get back to the cave entrance or a different one, if he could manage to find it.

So they ran on. Finally he saw it, something that looked familiar, a sharp left turn up ahead.

"C'mon!" he said with all the breath he could muster.

"I—am." Dusti responded.

They ducked into the small area, one he thought was too small for a horse, and then saw an even smaller opening down below. He knelt, lighting a match near the entrance. The flame bent towards it, indicating there was fresh air, or at least moving air, on the other side of it. They would have to crawl to get through and would also have to assume that the opening would get bigger, not smaller. He could not imagine having to crawl backwards out of such a space.

They also had to hope there were no unseemly creatures in there, waiting for them.

The hoofbeats drummed louder and louder, and then they started to fade. Perhaps the horseman, whoever or whatever it was, had passed them by or even given up on them.

Or it would be waiting on the other side of this wall. He had no idea.

"Dusti?" he said.

"Yes," she whispered.

"We have to try to go through here. It is a small opening. I hope it opens up more on the other side, but I have no idea. I think we have to try, though."

She bent forward over his lap and looked inside. "It is small."

As she sat back up, their eyes met, and she stopped, her face inches from his. She leaned in, kissing him hard on the lips. He kissed her back, and for a moment they shared passion, a fire. Then she broke the kiss.

"Thank you for getting us this far," she said. "I think I should go first."

"No, I—"

"Don't give me any of your macho bullshit. And really the main reason is that I am smaller. If we do have to back out, because it is too small of an opening for me, it will be easier that way. If not, I am sure I can handle whatever is on the other side as well as you can."

"You're probably right."

"Maybe better."

"You may be right about that, too," Kansas said.

"Good," she said. "Now that we've established that I am the leader, get out of my way."

Kansas moved the best he could, she pulled a flashlight from her pocket, and slid forward into the hole.

Seeing little choice, he followed.

It was immediately dark. He pulled out a light of his own, one he could barely manage to remove from his pocket, but he did not turn it on right away. He wanted to follow hers as long as he could, saving battery for one, and not alerting anyone who might see the lights for another.

Not that he thought that likely. And if someone was waiting on the other end, they wouldn't need to see a light to know they were coming.

He followed her boots, pushing along in an Army style crawl. He heard her grunt from time to time.

"Ouch," he heard her say. "Damn."

"You okay?" he asked.

"Yeah. Some of the rocks are a bit sharp, so watch yourself."

"Yep," he answered.

Then he felt one of them cut into his palm.

"Damn," he said.

"I told you so," she said, and he could hear a playful tone in her voice despite their serious situation.

He tried to watch himself. He made sure the uniform covered as much of his arms as possible, but as he scooted forward, it moved around, and he found it hard to keep it in place.

The rocks tore at the material and his skin, and he soon found that he was panting to keep up. The space did seem to be going on for a long time, and seemed to get narrower, too.

"Kansas?" Dusti said from up ahead.

"Yeah?"

"There is a narrow turn here. I can do it, but it might be tough for you. Also, watch out. I may have to kick a bit to get around."

"Okay."

"Once I am through, it looks like things open up a bit and I can probably turn around and help you through, too."

"I'm ready."

"I'm headed through," she said.

He backed up a little bit, as her boots kicked out, looking for purchase. With agonizing slowness, they moved away from her as she crawled around a corner. With her out of the way, he could see her concern. It was narrow, and a sharp, slightly less than 90 degree turn. If he got stuck in the middle, there would be no way to turn back, or to go forward without a lot of effort.

Or he might simply be stuck.

It was hard for him to move where he was, but he thought of what he might be able to shed to make himself smaller. The jacket might catch on the rocks, but it also might protect his skin. There was really nothing at all he could do without, except maybe the hat. A second later, he heard her squeal.

"I'm through. And not only does the cavern open up. You've got to see this."

"What is it?"

"You've got to see it. I can't explain it."

Kansas sighed and crawled forward.

Up close, the opening was even smaller than he thought. He turned on his own light, looking closely at the sharp edges.

This would be nearly impossible. He might need a stick of butter or something to grease him down to get through, even if he were not wearing a bulky uniform. But if he could get his shoulders through, he thought he would be fine.

So he pressed forward. He pushed his hat through, and he saw her hand reach out and grab it from the other side.

He thought for a second about the easiest way to make his shoulders smaller. He extended his hands forward like he was a swimmer diving into the water. With both hands extended in that pose he pushed forward with his legs.

He thought he would make it easily enough. He started to slide through, and then a rock on his right side caught the uniform.

With his hands at the odd angle in front of them, he had little strength to pull. He pushed with everything he could, but he needed something different, and with his legs at an angle around the corner, he couldn't figure anything out.

He was stuck.

He swiveled his head, halfway in and out of the hole, and decided to back out and try again. But when he tried to push back, he found himself unable to move more than an inch or two.

He should have removed the coat, taken the chance on a cut or scratch or two in order to get through. But he hadn't. He should have thought this through more, but he hadn't.

"Are you okay?" he heard Dusti say, the sound echoing to him.

"I'm stuck," he said. "Give me a minute."

The wool coat was tough. It would not rip easily. Going forward or back meant ripping the coat. Or maybe… He had an idea.

He pulled back a little, but not to the point where he was pulling on the coat.

"Dusti? Can you come here, crawl in where I can see you maybe?"

She did, and he saw her face up ahead, a look of concern showing she knew just how stuck he was.

"You see the problem, right?"

"You should have taken the jacket off?"

"Right. Thanks for pointing that out. So that's what I need you to do now."

"What?"

"Take the jacket off. I will stay right here, where I am not pulling on anything, and it is the loosest. I need you to pull it off, over my head."

"Okay. What if it gets stuck again?"

"Then it does, and we will have to deal with it."

"Um, I'll try." He saw her crawl forward and grab the sleeves at the wrist. She pulled.

The jacket shifted and caught. He tried to slip himself free, but it held him firmly. His hands were trapped, and he couldn't unbutton it. But what he could do was pull back.

As Dusti pulled on the sleeves, he worked his head backwards through the neck, and then pulled back, harder. His hands were now in the sleeves, and he had no way to grip anything at all. It would all depend on his legs and their strength.

So he pulled further, trying to slip rather than tug. If he could get his shoulders back through the opening, he would be home free.

He tried, and for a moment, he was stuck again. The jacket, although a lower part of it, was trapped between his shoulders and the rock. He pulled, gently, trying to squeeze his shoulders together, make them smaller.

Slowly, he moved against the cloth, his cotton t-shirt first sliding up and then dropping away. The wool was inches form his nose, and he felt like he was breathing nothing but the tickling and drying fibers.

He coughed, and as he did, he flew backward, something he could not do for any great distance, and struck the rock on the side of the tight tunnel.

The jacket slipped away, and he heard Dusti cry out in triumph.

"Think you can make it through now?"

"Just a minute," he said, taking the time to catch his breath. Then he put his hands back in the diving position and slipped through the hole.

He stopped for a second, fearful he was stuck yet again, but pulled in his shoulders one last time and slid through. Rocks dragged at his skin, leaving long scratches, but Dusti grabbed his hand and finished pulling him through.

A moment later, he was lying in a tunnel that was much larger than the one he had just left. He dragged himself forward with Dusti's help, and then he stood.

She handed him the uniform jacket back, and he slung it over his arm for now, surpassing a shiver.

After the warm confines of the passageway, this area was cold, and gooseflesh decorated his skin.

He then saw what Dusti had seen.

In the corner was a large, intricately carved wooden trunk. The lid was secured by a hasp and a large brass padlock.

They had found the treasure.

He let out a whoop and embraced her. Then he heard it, and the way she turned her head, he knew she'd detected the noise at the same time.

There was one passage leading out of this cavern holding the treasure besides the one they had crawled through. It was large, at least twelve feet high, and probably nearly as wide.

From the opening, they could hear the sound of approaching hoofbeats.

He looked back at the passage they had just left, with no desire to crawl back through it. From the pace of the approaching beast, they didn't have time anyway.

They were trapped. Just then, his phone chirped in his pocket, and he remembered the second part of his plan. He wondered if it would even matter now.

SEVENTEEN

The Horseman

C thulhu, Karen, and Davey Jones arrived at the overhang of rock and looked back. It appeared that their fight with Gestalt had not gone unnoticed, but some of the bystanders must have thought it was a part of the reenactment. Just before they entered the cut, Cthulhu looked back to hear a smatter of applause and see a few hearty souls out from under the cover of the awnings and the tree line.

He did the only thing he could think of to do, turned, and waved.

The applause got louder, and then he ducked under the overhang. He looked at the man sized crevasse, knowing what lay beyond, both the danger and the reward.

The sun had not yet set, but it might as well have. Would it be enough for the horseman to be active?

He gently set Karen down, and gently tapped her face with his hand once, twice, three times. She shook her head, and then opened her eyes.

"What happened?" she asked.

"We defeated Gestalt."

"Did I kill him?" She seemed genuinely horrified at the thought.

"No, but you did stab him. I finished him off, although—" He stopped mid-sentence. Had there been a spider, even a small one, who escaped? The dark and the rain might have obscured his view.

"A part of him may have survived," he finished. "But we are done hearing from him for now."

"I can't do this, Cthulhu."

"Do what?"

"Kill people—things. I can complain. Do things to further my own agenda. But I don't want to kill anyone or destroy them."

"And you don't have to. That is my job."

"Am I supposed to be okay with that?" she asked.

"I don't know," he told her honestly. "And we will have to talk about it later. For now, we are about to go somewhere, and I feel like I need to prepare you."

"Prepare me?"

"It is not what you are used to or likely have ever seen before. There are ghosts, as we talked about. I may have to talk to them in ways you don't understand. Just know this. As long as you are with me, you are safe. You understand me? Safe."

She nodded. "Cthulhu?"

"Yes, Karen?"

"Will you be okay?"

"Of course he will," Davey interjected. "But you two can knock the wacky romantic stuff off for now."

"We are just talking," Karen said, staring at him with a stern expression.

"Yeah," he said. "And while you are doing that, look who's coming." He pointed.

A group of uniformed shapes separated from the crowd. They looked almost like men, but something was off about each of them. Their shapes, the way they wore their hats, the unnatural gait each adopted.

They were awkward in their bodies, uncomfortable in their clothes and the weather, and they were, at a closer look, clearly not of this world.

"Already?" Cthulhu said.

Davey nodded. "They were likely already on the way. Your dispatching Gestalt accelerated things."

Davey was right. Cthulhu turned to Karen.

"You trust me, right?"

"Yes, as much as I trust anyone."

"Then get inside." He pushed her ahead of him into the crevasse, and before she could object, she staggered inside. He followed her, and Davey came last, struggling to get through the narrow opening.

He popped into the space a moment behind Cthulhu. He grabbed Karen's hand and turned right. "This way," he said.

In the distance he could hear the hooves of the horseman. He must be after Kansas and his companion. Good. The ghost would trap them, perhaps frighten them into running out of the caves, if they were not already lost.

Cthulhu quickened his step, and then heard something behind him, the rusting of cloth, the guttural sounds of the language of the Great Old Ones. He let out a sharp, shrill whistle.

He heard a distant neighing, one that sounded almost angry, and then the distant hoofbeats got louder.

"Will the horseman be able to handle them?" Davey asked.

"No. But he will delay them."

"What then?"

Cthulhu had a clever, slick, and utterly evil idea, one that might solve a number of problems all at once. But he chose to keep it to himself for the moment.

"We trap them," he said out loud.

"How?" Karen asked.

"Just leave that to me," he said.

They walked faster, and it became clear the horseman was getting closer.

"In here," he said, and they ducked into a small alcove in the wall barely big enough for two, let alone three. Davey squeezed in as close as he could, and Karen was pressed against Cthulhu in a pleasing yet slightly uncomfortable way.

The ethereal horse thundered by.

They stepped out behind them and walked quickly in the direction he'd come from. The temperature dropped as they walked, and they took several turns, each etched in Cthulhu's memory. He hated to think where they might have ended up had he not known the way.

Behind them, they heard the horseman neigh loudly, followed by shouts, grunts, and screams that were all the more horrifying for the distance they were away.

Karen panted and he turned to look at her. She looked overheated despite the cold, the red in her cheeks clearly visible due to her efforts.

"We're almost there," he told her.

"Good," she said. "You should complain to someone. They should make this journey easier. It's a long way to go for treasure."

"This is what keeps people away," he told her. "The effort makes it easy to keep the mortals from finding those things that are mine. Do you think men like Kansas shy away from effort when it comes to gold?"

"No," she answered. "It's just the inconvenience, that's all."

Cthulhu huffed, but she fell silent without the breath she would need to complain further. Cthulhu smiled. Even when she spoke against him, he loved it that she spoke her mind.

It was awful and adorable at the same time.

They rounded a final corner and there it was. An ornate wooden box, filled with intricate carvings and secured by a large brass padlock.

Karen stared in awe. "Do you have the key?"

Cthulhu pulled it from his pocket and smiled.

Davey stared too. "How long has it been since I laid eyes on such treasure?"

Cthulhu looked at him. "Too long, my friend."

"We'll take that," he heard a voice behind him. He turned to see Kansas, a torn union coat at his feet, in a white t-shirt and wearing an intricate union uniform hat.

His infamous whip was uncoiled, much of it laying in a deadly coil at his side, the handle in his hand.

Next to him was a woman who looked vaguely familiar. She held a pistol, pointed steadily at him.

Cthulhu just smiled, and he heard Karen snarl next to him.

"Who the hell are you?" Davey Jones said.

"This, Davey, is Kansas Smith and a—new companion? They are going to help us get out of here."

"Why would we do that?" Kansas asked.

"Because if you do, I will offer you two things. I'll let you live. And I'll give you a nice percentage of this."

"Why don't we just take it all ourselves?" the new woman asked.

"Because once we're out of here, I'll tell you where you can find more. Much more."

"In trade?"

"You leave me alone. Me, my new friend Karen, and our companion Davey here. We'll do the same for you."

"What makes you think we will trust you?"

"Because," Davey said quietly. "If you don't, I'll blow a hole in you a mile wide."

Kansas turned to look, and saw his friend had a short musket pistol. But it was clearly cocked, loaded, and deadly.

Kansas looked at the woman with him. "Maybe we can come to an understanding."

A scream, a roar, and a guttural yell interrupted them.

"We better reach it fast," Cthulhu said. "Or the Great Old Ones will kill us all."

"This was your plan?" Karen said.

"It's the only choice we have," Cthulhu said. "Well? Will you join us in life so we can help each other? Or will you join us in death, and let our common enemy overrun us?"

Kansas stared him down, and then another roar came from the tunnel. Cthulhu put out his hand. Kansas took it.

"Great," Cthulhu said. "We have only a few moments to get our defense and our plan together before they are on us."

"I'm listening," Kansas said.

Cthulhu issued his instructions like a commander with an authority that indicated he was not to be disobeyed.

The others moved into their places while he stood directly blocking any view of the treasure chest from the tunnel opening.

He really hoped this would work. Otherwise, he would be returned to the land of the Great Old Ones, Idh-yaa might end up with more than half of his stuff after all, and he might never see Karen again.

That thought alone inspired him to harden his defenses. He grew just a little beyond his current form, stretching the uniform he wore to its limited, and set both of his feet shoulder width apart.

He heard the loud neighing of the horseman behind the grunts and groans of the approaching enemy.

They had no idea they were the ones surrounded and trapped. If only he could send them back where they belonged without being dragged with them.

He took a deep breath and roared his anger with everything he had as the first of their opponents rounded the corner.

KANSAS HAD no intention of trusting Cthulhu, but he also didn't want to die. He wondered what the big creature was thinking, but he'd kept the human with her. He hadn't eaten her, torn her asunder, or sent her packing. That had to mean either he really was in some kind of love, whatever form of that he was capable of, or she had some kind of hold on him.

But the monster seemed mellower, more logical than he expected. There was no time to think about it now.

The first creature from the world of the Great Old Ones entered the small corridor. Their bulk and clumsiness in human form seemed to play against them, but the space was small, and Kansas understanding of their ability to change form, even slightly, was that it took a lot of energy and effort.

And time.

They had that on their side.

Cthulhu brushed the creature aside with a large arm, and it struck the wall and fell. Raspy screams came from its throat.

Another creature emerged, heading straight for Karen. Kansas uncoiled his whip, lashed out and wrapped the end around its arm.

He pulled, and the arm split in half, a large part of it falling to the floor. Thick, black blood pooled at its feet.

The creature roared, and he could see the flesh trying to knit together and heal, but the beast slid down against the wall, sitting on the floor.

He'll be back, Kansas thought. And he'll be pissed. But not before we can end this thing.

He turned his head and saw yet another creature roaring through the gap. Beyond him, a larger beast was wrestling with Cthulhu, the two of them shoving each other back and forth, neither able to topple the other.

It was white, pale white like Gestalt had been, but taller and more muscular. It's uniform, a confederate one, hung in gray tatters around its waist.

He pulled the whip back to him, and faced it, but before he could strike, the creature went down in a blur. A moment later, Davey was straddling his chest, and pulled the classic musket pistol. The creature's face disappeared in a spray of the same black blood.

The man's quickness astonished him, until he remembered that while he might look like a portly man, he was not a man at all.

He heard Cthulhu roar, and the creature he'd been wrestling with flew toward them.

"Look out!" he yelled, but Dusti was on it already. She slipped to the side, and as the creature hit the wall and then the ground, she was on it, shooting it with a much more conventional pistol with the same effect.

The body shimmered and disappeared.

He turned to see the other body had done the same. The creature he'd torn the arm from was nowhere to be found.

Another roar came from the tunnel, but it seemed to be headed the other direction down the tunnel. Cthulhu ran after it. He heard a thud, and then nothing.

Then the large, greenish skinned creature returned.

He folded his arms and smiled. "We did it. I thought surely they would send more soldiers than that."

"Cthulhu?" Davey asked.

"Yes?"

"What happened to the horseman?"

"The—?" He cocked his head, and like the obedient followers they were, Kansas saw everyone else do the exact same thing. In fact, he tilted his own head, straining to hear.

The hoofbeats, once a dominant sound in the space, were gone. There was only silence.

Uncomfortable, eerie silence.

Cthulhu's tentacles face went from a smile to a confused frown, an odd look for him.

Then Kansas remembered something else. Just before the group had arrived, he'd sent out a Tweet. "He's here. #CthulhuinGettysburg Find him at the Devil's Den."

He'd not only led the Great Old Ones to him, but he'd probably also incited his followers to another rally.

They would disrupt the reenactment, which might already be going on, but they would also give any second wave of Great Old Ones a solid target.

"What?" Cthulhu asked him.

"What do you mean, what?" Kansas said. Dusti moved to his side.

"You did something," the up-until-now silent Karen said. "What is it?"

"I—um—" Kansas stopped and sighed. The problem was he'd put them all in danger, and they needed to know what he'd done in order to make it right. "You might want to check Twitter."

Slowly, she took out a large phone, one that looked more like a piece of toast than a communications device.

She swiped to open the device and the screen lit up.

"What in the world?" She turned the screen toward him, and he took a couple of hesitant steps forward. Dusti was on his arm.

There was nothing there.

He opened his own phone and social media app.

"Your tweet has been removed because it contained inappropriate content," the screen read.

Then he paused. He heard something, distant, but growing louder.

Two hour roars came from deep in the cavern. Followed by loud hoofbeats.

His Tweet may have been removed, but maybe not in time.

"Get ready," Cthulhu said.

Karen stepped up next to him. She opened a large bag, almost a suitcase, and pulled out a large pistol.

Kansas and Dusti stepped up beside them the best they could, and Davey joined them. They formed a human wall in the cavern in front of the large chest.

He looked back at it again, wondering what exactly this treasure contained, how Cthulhu knew Davey, and how this would all shake out.

Then the attack began, and there was no more time for thinking.

This time the creatures came not one at a time, but en masse. Soon he saw the reason why.

They were being chased. There were at least two dozen off them, and suddenly the chamber and the tunnel leading to it were a scene of chaos.

A creature leapt for him, one that looked to be part cougar, part bull. It had giant horns and the gaping mouth of a mountain cat. He struck it down with the whip and coiled for another strike, taking two small steps back.

He glimpsed another similar creature landing on Dusti, and a muffled gunshot sounded. The creature fell to the ground, shimmered, and disappeared.

Ahead of them, he saw the horseman in the distance behind them. Although ghostly and nearly transparent, the horse reared, and its hooves tore into a creature at the rear of the charge. The being immediately disappeared in a glitter filled shimmer, as if it had been beamed away by a Star Trek like transporter.

None of the creatures who disappeared seemed to reappear.

Cthulhu strode forward, tearing into the creatures, sending some flying, grabbing some of the smaller creatures and tearing their bodies in half. Karen was firing what looked to be a revolver, one too large for her hands, but that she seemed to handle expertly.

Five creatures fell, one on top of the other, in a spray of blood and flesh, then the entire pile shimmered and disappeared.

Davey moved with size-defying speed, cutting through several creatures at once. Another broke through their lines, this one looking like a possessed unicorn with a long, giraffe like neck. Kansas flicked the whip, and it wrapped around its neck, then seemed to disappear into the flesh and cut right through. He pulled, and much like the arm of the creature earlier, the head separated from the body. It struck him in his gut and knocked him back. The back of his thighs struck something, and he felt himself go over backward. As he did, he saw the ghostly horseman enter the chamber and rear again.

Instinctively, Kansas grabbed the head in his lap, and then he felt his own head strike the rock of the wall. Just before he blacked out, he saw he'd tripped over the treasure chest.

Then he felt pain, an odd lightness come over his hand, and heard an odd screeching sound. Then there was nothing.

EIGHTEEN

The Final Battle

C thulhu felt the first wave of assailants, and with it came a certain rage. He knew that these creatures would not die but would merely return to the Land of the Great Old Ones, but he wanted to ensure that they arrived with a message.

Don't mess with Cthulhu and his friends.

Were he to decide to stay here, he would have to talk to the council of course, but he wanted a strong argument for them to let him do what he wanted.

So he tore into them. He slammed some into walls, tore others in half. He heard Karen's weapon sound at least five times, and grinned. She was indeed a force to be reckoned with.

Kansas and his woman friend also did well. The woman sent several creatures packing with her small pistol and her own fighting skills, and he grinned. Perhaps he would let them live after all. This truce would be a necessary thing to honor were he to live here on this earth for any length of time at all.

Davey was the biggest surprise of all in the battle. His speed and agility astounded Cthulhu, and he wondered if he had taken on the cumbersome human form he had for that reason. The creatures underestimated him time and time again, and he tore through them with no mercy.

The horseman was at the rear and seemed to be keeping the creatures from running or escaping. Somehow his ethereal hooves tore into these creatures, and several died at his feet. He swung a nearly invisible sword, and it too seemed to cut as cleanly as a physical one.

Cthulhu roared in pleasure, then looked back. He saw Kansas fall after tripping on the trunk, and hitting the wall with a sickening crunch.

The woman ran toward him, and Cthulhu was distracted, only for a moment.

"Behind you!" Karen screamed.

But it was too late. A creature closed in on him, and Cthulhu narrowly avoided a swipe from its blade. He danced away and swung at the creature with a free arm. It ducked, and Cthulhu saw what it was.

The humans called them ogres. It was ugly, the type of ugly that made Cthulhu's tentacled face look like a beauty queen. Three horns protruded from the top of its head. They were small and stubby, disfiguring at best. Its eyes were perched at the bottom of the slope of a massive and wrinkled forehead. It's mouth protruded beyond the seemingly crushed nose struggling for existence on the dry desert of its face.

Its chin thrusted out much further, and pointed teeth stuck out in a deadly underbite.

Cthulhu roared, and swung again, and the creature grabbed his arm with stubby hands of its own. Cthulhu pulled back, and the creature came with him, but his jaws opened wide, wider than it should have been possible, and clamped down on flesh.

Cthulhu roared in pain and watched in horror as his hand dropped away. The creature fell to the ground and Cthulhu stomped his foot down on its neck.

It disappeared with a grin.

Now one armed, Cthulhu turned to see what would be next. There were four creatures advancing on him. He glanced left and right.

Davey was still there, panting but standing ready to fight. Beyond and behind him, Kansas' woman stood, but more guarding the chest and her fallen friend than defending everyone.

To his right, Karen stood. She looked pale but determined, her large pistol steady and prepared.

This was it, the last stand. He looked at his damaged right arm.

The flesh was healing, a new extension of his arm, a tentacle really, already formed.

But it would be much too late. He remembered the sword Davey had given him, and he drew it awkwardly with his left hand.

And roared.

The sound echoed through the chamber, seeming to shake rocks lose from the ceiling and the surrounding walls. Gravel rained down around him, and the horseman neighed, turned, and ran the other direction.

But his companions stood fast, as did the creatures from the Underworld.

The first lunged, and Cthulhu cut him. It wasn't enough, and the creature came on.

A gunshot sounded from beside him and the creature exploded. Karen whooped in triumph.

"Karen!" Davey cried.

Cthulhu looked toward her, and time slowed. One of the creatures approached her, another ogre, jaws wide. If she were bitten she would not shimmer and disappear. She would not heal as he did. She would die.

He roared, but the falling body of the creature she'd killed tripped him as he moved toward her.

She pulled the trigger on the pistol.

Click. Click. She pulled again. Click.

She was out. She screamed and pulled the weapon back, striking the creature between the eyes.

Time slowed. It stopped moving forward, staggered, and it's odd eyes glazed for a second.

It was only that second that mattered, because in a single step, Davey was there. He grabbed the creature and tried to stab it with his sword.

But even dazed the monster was too quick. The blow had been strong, but not enough to take it out completely. It ducked and turned toward his friend.

Cthulhu struggled to rise but felt something heavy on him. He looked at his arm, slowly healing, and realized it was sapping all his energy.

"Get—" the cry died in his throat, as another creature appeared blocking his view. It raised a heavy, odd looking sword.

Then a hole appeared in its head. Kansas' woman moved forward, and then shot it again.

The creature shimmered and disappeared. Just in time for him to see Davey and the ogre.

The creature shoved his friend and then bent down, moving to bite his neck. Davey took the sword he had and shoved it through creature's middle.

At the same time the creature's teeth closed on Davey's jugular vein. Cthulhu saw it happen, unable to stop it. And he knew what would come next.

"No!" he roared.

But both Davey and the creature disappeared with a shimmer.

Davey Jones was gone.

Cthulhu turned his head and saw one final creature running towards him. Hoofbeats sounded through the stone next to his ear, and he tried to rise. The horseman was right behind it.

Then the whip came out of the darkness. Kansas was up and moving.

The creatures head disappeared in a spray, and then its body fell. Something hard struck Cthulhu's head, and the last thing he saw before he blacked out was the horseman standing in front of Kansas, Karen, and the new woman.

The creature shimmered, its weight leaving his chest, but his eyes closed despite his best attempts to keep them open.

KANSAS WOKE TO SEE A DISASTER. Several creatures had disappeared, but Karen stood, clearly in shock. Dusti was not far away, her pistol pointed at a creature. He heard the click of a firing pin on an empty chamber.

So he stood as quickly as he could and lashed out with his whip. The large, ogre like creature fell on Cthulhu, shimmered and disappeared, but the tentacle faced creature didn't move.

His eyes were closed. Kansas could see part of his arm was missing but seemed to be regrowing.

He raced forward. Davey was nowhere to be seen. The horse-man, a ghostly, ethereal form stood in front of Dusti and Karen, and he joined them.

It was his first chance to get a good look at the creature. The horse itself was huge, reminiscent of the Budweiser Clydes-dales, but a little smaller. Maybe more like a Bud Light.

Speaking of which, the creature appeared to be silver, or at least silver-gray. It's almost transparent saddle contained a creature that was, well, odd to say the least. It was a squat man, whose legs nearly stuck out they were so short. It held the reins but didn't seem to pull on them or direct the horse at all.

And when he looked up, he saw it had no head.

Then he looked again. It's head was in its hand.

And the head seemed to stare at him. Then it spoke.

"You do not belong here."

"I don't—look, you have no head."

"Yes, I do."

"Well, it's off. Not on your shoulders."

The arm lifted the head, apparently so it could look at itself.

"Well, so it is. That has no bearing on your presence here."

"We're with him," he said, pointing to Cthulhu.

Karen nodded, but her eyes were empty.

Dusti seemed better, but still not one-hundred percent.

What did he expect? His own head ached, but he was literally having a conversation with a headless horseman.

"Cthulhu and the great Davey Jones have tasked me with protecting their treasure. Until he tells me otherwise, whoever attempts to take it must die."

"Davey Jones? As in Davey Jones's locker?"

"Oh, no," the horseman said. "This is Davey Jones, Jr. He never amounted to what his father was. Always a bit of a slacker, that one."

"Um, okay."

"Enough talk!" the head roared. "Who wants to die first?"

"Excuse me," Karen said. "What gives you the right to determine who lives and dies."

"Well, I am the horseman, charged with protecting the treasure."

"And who selected this cave anyway. It's drafty and chilly. Can't you turn up the heat?"

"The heat? Ma'am, the——"

"Ma'am?" Karen said. "Ma'am? Who do you think you are talking to?"

"Listen, um, whatever your name is. I am just charged with protecting the treasure in this cave. I don't really control the temperature or much else actually. I'm kind of a ghost, in case you haven't noticed."

"I see. So you are not in charge?"

"Well, not exactly. I mean—"

"So who is, Mr. Headless Horseman?"

"It's complicated—"

"Complicated? How complicated can a drafty old cave be? I want to talk to your supervisor."

"My supervisor?" The arm holding the head swung it around, looking at itself and then around the cave.

Dusti laughed.

"What are you laughing at?"

"She can laugh if she wants. Look at me!" Karen commanded.

"Okay, okay." The head swung back her way.

"Your supervisor. Your manager. Whoever that is, I want to talk to them. Now. No one is just going to kill me in some cavern until I get some answers."

"Well, I—gee. I have no idea who to talk to."

The stallion snorted.

"Figure it out," Karen said. "No one is going to die here until you do."

Kansas laughed too as she folded her arms. What had seemed like a serious situation was now almost funny.

Then he heard a voice from behind them.

"No one is dying today, Ian. Get lost," Cthulhu said.

"Yes, sir," the horseman said. He turned to go.

"Wait!" Karen said. "He owes me an apology."

Cthulhu stepped forward and looked at the three of them, and then at the horseman. "Well?"

"Sorry," the horseman said. His free hand released the reins, removed the hat from his head, and doffed it to her. "I had no idea who you were and who you were with. Please accept my apology."

"Done," Karen said.

The horse ran off, the hoofbeats fading as it did.

Karen turned and embraced Cthulhu. Kansas watched for a second, and then turned to Dusti.

"Thanks for everything," he told her.

"Everything?" she answered, a twinkle in her eye.

"You know, saving my life and all that."

"Oh, yes," she said. "Of course."

He smiled. "So, we are going to have a helluva payday here."

"Looks like it, as long as Cthulhu keeps his word."

"I always keep my word," he said.

Kansas turned to look and saw the creature and Karen arm in arm. "But this truce is permanent. I will, however, give you a clue."

"A clue?"

"The location of another treasure. This one further west. That one, should you find it, you can have completely."

Kansas looked at Dusti, and then back to Cthulhu. "The price?"

"Only our truce. And one other thing."

"Yes?"

"I may be sticking around for a while. So should I need your help with a similar problem in the future, you need to be available."

"Deal."

"Now, let's get this thing open." Cthulhu took a key from his pocket and inserted it in the lock.

With a click it fell away. He lifted the heavy lid with his one good hand.

The trunk was filled with rubies, gold, emeralds, treasure beyond anything Kansas had ever seen.

"How much can I take?" he asked breathlessly.

"We take," Dusti corrected.

"As much as you can carry," Cthulhu said.

Dusti looked at him, and both took heavy canvas bags from their pockets.

Then Kansas heard another voice from behind them.

"You dividing up my treasure without me?"

He turned and saw Davey Jones, Jr. standing there.

"Davey!" Cthulhu said. "I thought you were—"

"Nope. I managed to make it back through the door they opened into this world, not far from here. Then I closed it behind me."

"That's amazing!"

"Well you know what they say."

"What's that?" Karen asked him with a smile.

"When a god closes a door, he opens a window."

"A window?"

Davey walked to the back of the chamber and pressed a small area on the stone. A panel slid aside, revealing a stone window of sorts with a low ledge.

"A window," he said. "The way out."

The five of them all filled large bags with treasure, as heavy as they could pack them.

"Can we come back for more later?" Dusti asked.

"Nope. That's it for this treasure, at least for the next hundred years or so," Cthulhu said.

She didn't ask why, but Kansas watched as she added a few more rubies to her bag.

Kansas and Dusti hefted their bags of treasure and went first. Davey followed. Cthulhu and Karen came last, also equally laden.

When Kansas ducked his head out, a cheer went up from the gathered crowd.

The rain had stopped, and the battle in front of them fumbled and then stopped. They were atop the rocks of the Devil's Den and interspersed with the soldiers was a whole crowd of people with picket signs and wearing t-shirts.

"Cthulhu for President, 2024."

"This is my President."

"The Chaos Party."

"The Greatest of all the Evils."

"Well," Kansas said. "Looks like your fans found you. At least now you have the funding to run a campaign."

"Sure, sure," Cthulhu said, waving absently.

"There is the matter of the birth certificate," Dusti joked.

"I can take care of that," Karen said. "I know the birth certificate manager in North Carolina."

Kansas smiled, and looked at the ridiculous group one more time.

"I guess this is where we part ways," he said.

"At least for now," Cthulhu said. "Thank you Kansas."

In shock, Kansas took his hand, shook it and walked away.

Dusti took his hand as they walked down the hill away from the battlefield toward where they were parked, large canvas bags weighing them down as they went.

"Did that just happen?" Dusti said.

"Yep."

"Where to now?"

Kansas unfolded a piece of paper Cthulhu had handed him.

He turned to her. "South Dakota," he said. "Looks like we have another treasure to find. Assuming you are sticking with me, that is?"

"Of course," she said, reaching up and kissing him on the cheek. "Now, let's get back to the hotel. I believe we were interrupted earlier."

Kansas grinned, and sped up his pace. He'd found treasure and the woman of his dreams. Who could ask for anything more?

NINETEEN

The Manager

C thulhu and Karen made it through the crowd of fans and reenactors alike, and then made their way with Davey back to his place, where they dropped him off. They then headed back to their hotel.

"I feel like we should celebrate," Cthulhu said.

"Oh, we will," she said. "Leave it to me."

They walked into the hotel lobby. A thin man, one who looked oddly familiar, stood at the desk. On his chest, next to an odd looking tie, was a black name tag with his name on it, and below that the moniker, "Manager."

He looked up at the couple and smiled.

"How can I help you?" he said.

"Well, our room is a bit of a problem," Karen said. "The bed is not comfortable, and the shower is much too small," she said, indicating Cthulhu. "We would like an upgrade."

"Let me see what we have," he said, and his hands clicked over keyboard keys.

"Well?" Karen asked impatiently.

"We do have a honeymoon suite. There is a jetted tub, and a king sized bed. It comes with a complimentary bottle of champagne."

"That sounds great."

"Do you want to charge the difference to the card on file? We can even move your luggage and things for you."

"Charge it?"

"Yes, ma'am. The difference is—"

"Difference? I just told you our room was not to our satisfaction. I assumed you would be giving us the upgrade."

"Well, I can't just upgrade you for—"

"You are a manager, are you not?"

"I am."

"Then you can upgrade us for free. I know you can."

"Well, I'm not sure—"

"Do I need to speak with your supervisor?"

Cthulhu watched in awe as she cajoled and manipulated the manger, and a few moments later they had a room upgrade and a voucher for their next visit.

As they turned to walk away, Cthulhu looked back at the manager. The man was scowling at them. He started walking and saw a large spider in front of him. It was odd, with red eyes. He stepped on it and kept going. He didn't want Karen to see it and have her file yet another complaint. He wanted to get her up to the hotel room where they could spend some more time alone.

He still had to decide what to do next, but for now he planned to stay and see how things worked out. Maybe he could run for president after all. Maybe there was a loophole he could find.

They reached the elevator, and she turned to him.

"So, what are you going to do next?"

He shrugged. "I'm staying, if that's what you mean. What comes after that, I don't know. Maybe a presidential run, maybe just more hi-jinks on the high seas."

"That sounds amazing. I've always wanted to take one of those crappy cruises so I can complain about it."

"Sounds perfect to me."

They rode up to their new room in silence.

Karen opened the door and stepped inside first. The room was much larger, with a seating area. A bottle of champagne waited for them in a bucket of ice. He walked around, looked at the large screen TV, and then headed for the bathroom. A huge jetted tub, perhaps big enough for four, waited there. Karen started the water, testing it with her elbow and waiting for it to fill.

There was no chemical smell, nothing that would harm his skin. Cthulhu started to undress.

Karen stopped him.

"Here, let me," she said. She slowly unbuttoned the civil ware uniform, dropping it to the floor. He returned the favor, helping her out of her now ruined and stained dress. She slipped into the water.

"Why don't you get the champagne?" she said.

He walked out to the table, grabbed it and two glasses, and returned to the bathroom. He popped the cork on the bottle and poured the golden liquid into the two flutes provided.

She gestured to him, and he joined her in the water, slipping in and letting the warmth of it and her flow through him.

Cthulhu was happy. He wasn't sure he liked it, but he didn't not like it either.

As he moved across the tub to kiss her, Karen met him in the middle. She reached over, grabbed the glasses and handed one to hm.

"To us," she said.

"To us," he agreed.

He'd never felt better in his entire life.

Epilogue

Deadwood, South Dakota Six Months Later

"Who knew it could be so cold here?" Dusti said.

"Well, they do have winter here. What did you expect?" Kansas said.

"Who would hide treasure in Deadwood. I mean, look at all these casinos?"

"It wasn't always like this."

"Where do we start?"

"Well, I think we start in our hotel room," he told her. "We can go out in the hills tomorrow. Tonight we feast, drink, and gamble."

"Gamble?"

"Only a little. We can afford it."

She smiled, and he knew it was because he was right. He'd found a buyer for their first treasure, and they had some of the most state of the art equipment in the world now.

Tomorrow, if they were successful, they would be nearly as rich as Elon Musk, minus the space travel and electric cars.

They stepped up to the hotel desk.

"We have a reservation," he said. "Kansas Smith and Dusti Rhodes."

The clerk, a thin man with thick glasses, an unfortunate mustache, and a tag that read manager, checked them in quickly.

"Here are your keys," he said pleasantly. "Room 214. Let me know if we can get you anything."

They took the keys and walked away. As they did, Kansas thought he saw a large spider scurry under the desk.

Bit cold for spiders, he thought. *But maybe they just find their way inside in the winter here.*

He ignored it, put his arm around Dusti and led her toward their room. Hopefully this adventure would be much less exciting than the one in Gettysburg.

But you never could tell.

Moving Forward: On to Book 2: Coming Early 2022

About the Author

Denise Lynn Lambert is an emerging romantic comedy author, and her debut, *The Call of Karen*, is her first full length novel.

Denise is a dog lover, a lover of books, and lives in the great state of Idaho, although that is about as specific as she'll get. Someday she would love to have a winter home in the Caribbean or somewhere warm, with sand and a nice beach.

Made in the USA
Middletown, DE
13 June 2023

32508503R00142